SỌCHIMA

AWAKENING

OF

THE GODS

SỌCHIMA

AWAKENING

OF

THE GODS

UCHECHI THERESA EZEUKO

This book is dedicated to my father, Chief
OKEY SOLOMON OKPALUGOH,
Omenife Achina,

and

my father-in-law, Late **CHARLES
IFEDIBALUCHUKWU EZEUKO,**

both lovers of tradition.

A Fastide Production series

ISBN: 978-0-9948277-6-0

PROLOGUE

Royalty was a thing of pride, fame, and power. For the Ubaka dynasty, it was something that should remain in the family for as long as it can stay.

However, the price of staying was all dependent on the birth of an heir to succeed the throne.

A long-lasting tradition which had a time stamp on it. After ten years of marital bliss between kings and their queens, if a male heir were yet to be conceived, the royal rights would shift to another family in line to the throne. This tradition had existed over five hundred years ago as the royal rights circulated within the clan of Ezeuwa, whose lineage kept producing heirs.

Nevertheless, in fairness, the kingdom of Ogbodo finally agreed in unison and in accordance with the traditions of the land. They decided to implement a ten-year time stamp to give each royal family a chance to rule the great kingdom of Ogbodo.

Ogbodo kingdom was richly blessed with palm fruits and good harvest. People from neighbouring towns would travel far and wide to conduct trade business with the merchants of Ogbodo kingdom. Kingship in the land was quite satisfying and a treasure to die for.

The Ubaka dynasty was in no doubt of their royal rights and was willing to keep it forever. However, for king Obeze and his queen, it was the beginning of a new era in their reign, and, whether the gods liked it or not, continuity is somewhat guaranteed, by any means possible.

CHAPTER ONE

Prince Obeze woke up, stretching his arms and yawning instantaneously. Yesterday had been tiring, the full day spent deliberating and consulting with the gods of Ogbodo kingdom. All he had wanted after was a good night's sleep.

The responsibilities of kingship had burdened his mind as he had taken the last cleansing rite of an heir apparent. He would be king should anything befall his father, King Chigbo, the great king of Ogbodo kingdom.

Prince Obeze sighed heavily as the thought of his predicament raced through his mind in swift torrent. The morning is here, and the day is filled with its uncertainties and expectations, Prince Obeze thought.

The prince got up and strolled towards the door, grabbing his clay cup. He poured palm wine from the clay tote. He carefully placed the calabash of palm wine on the floor and settled into his wooden rocking chair at the far end of the huge verandah.

Prince Obeze silently prayed: Gods of Ogbodo kingdom, my days are fading fast! Fast enough to deny me the kingship of this kingdom. The day brings light, but the loneliness and emptiness have cursed my heart. When will I ever have children? It's been nine years already since I married Obiageli! When shall a baby's cry fill the emptiness that I feel? Prince Obeze gazed up to the sky in thought.

He was desperate for an answer, yet the gods remained silent.

 "My lord, what burdens your feelings at this early hour?" Obiageli asked as she emerged from her chambers, looking disturbed at the mere sight of Prince Obeze.

"And why is my queen up so early?" Prince Obeze smiled at his wife, who could tell the reason for his thoughts!

"I can bet with my life that you haven't slept a wink all night," Prince Obeze said as he looked at Obiageli curiously. He hugged her as she pressed her head against his chest while sobbing quietly.

She closed her eyes for a moment and held her breath, ensuring she hid her watery eyes.

"Do not try to hide the tears, my love. I know you are sobbing; I can feel your tears piercing my heart," Prince Obeze whispered into Obiageli's ear.

"For how long, my lord? How long are we going to continue living like this?" Obiageli asked as she freely let the tears wet Prince Obeze's chest. "We have only a year left. If we have no child after ten years of marriage, then we have no heir, and the kingship leaves our reign. That has always been the tradition of our land."

Obeze nodded; she was right, but he did not know how to solve their problem.

"Is there anything our king, your father, can do to avert such cruel traditions?" Obiageli asked, grabbing onto Obeze with a desperate moan of frustration and futility.

"It's the tradition, my love. The tradition was there long before our forefathers," Prince Obeze replied with a stab of disappointment.

Obiageli tried to avoid Prince Obeze's eyes penetrating deep into her own.

Obiageli broke away from Obeze's grip in anger. "King Chigbo Ubaka is your father and king. Soon, he may join his ancestors, my love. If that happens, you will lose the kingship because we have no heir! We must do something! I do not want you to lose the throne of your father because of my childlessness."

"And who told you childlessness is the fault of the woman alone?" Prince

Obeze challenged, trying to conceal his agitation.

"We are in this together, and we will get through it together!" Prince Obeze assured Obiageli as he stroked her face. He pulled her into his arms, brushing his hands against her hair.

"My husband, whose weight I carry in between my thighs, I love you," Obiageli whispered as she tightened her grip around Obeze's waist. As footsteps approached, Obiageli and Prince Obeze disentangled from their embrace. Obeze cleared his throat and reached for his cup of palm wine, while Obiageli adjusted her wrapper neatly wrapped around her breasts as she made her way back to her chambers.

As the footsteps approached closer, Prince Obeze flung the door open to see Obika, the king's guard, approaching. Dressed in his brown khaki shorts with his shoes tied messily, Obika swung his sword under his right armpit.

"Who do you seek at this hour? Is my father, the king, alright?" Prince Obeze asked suspiciously.

"Long live my prince," Obika responded with a head bow. "Your father, our king, summons you."

"Thank you, Obika; tell my father I shall be with him soon," Prince Obeze said with a hand wave as he walked back into his chambers.

Ezemmuo, the chief priest of Ogbodo kingdom, arrived at the king's palace. His sad look made King Chigbo Ubaka worried and perplexed.

"What is it that awakens the messenger of the gods so early that I can see and hear the ferociousness in your chants?" King Ubaka asked. He ushered Ezemmuo inside the throne room.

"Time is running out, my king," Ezemmuo blurted, with a stern look. He looked down at the divination mat, picked up a piece of white chalk, and drew a big circle on a piece of red cloth lying on the mat.

"My king, you know the tradition of the land. Obeze your son must have an heir to ascend the throne!" This is a guarantee that the kingship lineage will continue with the Ubaka dynasty. The ancestral timeframe is ten years! Obeze has been married for nine years!"

The king listened intently, looking worried.

"The gods have spoken!" Ezemmuo concluded as he sat down on the divination mat. His words of incantation resonated in the room.

King Chigbo Ubaka heaved a sigh of distress and anxiety. He asked, "Ezemmuo, the great messenger of the gods, are the gods offended? Has my son done something wrong to suffer for his childlessness? Why have the gods remained silent on this issue?"

Ezemmuo stood up abruptly while thinking about what the king had just said. He nodded his head and cleared his throat in his typical way. Carrying his old brown bag, he slowly and carefully made his way to the exit.

He turned to the king shakily. "The gods have spoken! I am only a messenger; I cannot question their thoughts."

Ezemmuo left the king's palace, but not without bumping into Prince Obeze who was walking to the king's throne room. Obeze threw a stern but confused look at Ezemmuo. He watched as the old chief priest made his way to the outside of the courtyard.

"Father, what brings Ezemmuo here at this early hour?" Obeze asked as he bowed before his father.

The king remained silent while looking away.

"You sent for me, Father," Obeze said as he tried to interrupt his father's thoughts. Obeze knew his father was worried about his childlessness but he did not imagine that would be a topic open for discussion at such early hour of the morning.

"The gods remain silent, my son," the king muttered in a trembling voice. Obeze reached for his father's hand, leaning closer to his chair.

"Father, your health has not been good lately, and you should not burden your heart with my childlessness," Obeze warned. Carefully, he removed the beads from the king's neck. Obeze lifted the crown from the king's head and placed it carefully on the table beside the throne. The king coughed while trying to drink from his carved ceramic cup.

"My son, if only the gods had spoken, we would know the cause of the issue at hand. Then we would make the sacrifice needed to cleanse the family from this great problem." King Ubaka concluded with a weak sigh and handed the ceramic cup to Obeze.

"Get some rest, Father," Obeze added as he carefully placed the cup on the side table. He did not have much to say when the king's health was failing.

"Thank you, my son," King Chigbo replied as he made his way back to his chambers.

CHAPTER TWO

King Chigbo Ubaka had been the ruler and king of Ogbodo kingdom for more than two decades.

He took over from his father, King Udodi Ubaka the Great, after he had died of a mysterious illness.

No one knew the cause of his ailment, not even the great Ujankita from the tribe of Awoja. King Udodi Ubaka suffered greatly for five years from the ailment before joining his ancestors. Belief had it that the Ubaka clan was suffering from an unknown curse, which no priest or priestess had been able to change.

King Chigbo Ubaka was barely a boy growing into a young man when his father died. He just wanted to be a child and to not to be burdened with the leadership of a kingdom. They say that destiny and fate have a way of turning things around, and the young boy began to learn the ways of kingship.

One can argue that the timing for Chigbo Ubaka to become king, at the age of sixteen, was good, since that age was the prime of youth, when young men were introduced into the manhood initiation rites. After the rites, they are believed to be ready to have children.

King Chigbo Ubaka ruled the people just like his father did. He was a man of very few words, but his words urged moral discipline and adherence to law and tradition. However, being a king at an early age came with a price: the pressure of finding a bride to bear a male child so that the royal lineage could continue.

Experiencing the rites of manhood initiation was a tormenting life phase for the young men of Ogbodo, who must all face the trials at the age of sixteen. It was a dramatic experience and a tradition that must be upheld. The purpose was to determine if the men were fertile enough to be given away in marriage. Being certified as fertile increased the chances of a child after a man took a bride. No woman wanted to be married off to a man who never took part in the manhood initiation ceremony.

This ceremonial act was done by rubbing the manhood against both palms with palm oil smeared on each palm. They would have to rub hard until an ejaculation happened. While this was going on, the chief priest would offer sacrifices to the gods of fertility. With prayers to nourish the sperm and fill it with both male and female children.

The birth of Prince Obeze was a blessing for King Chigbo Ubaka and his queen, Nnedi Ubaka.

Through Prince Obeze, it seemed the Ubaka dynasty would continue to rule. If he produced no heir, however, the fair tradition would mean that the kingship passed to another clan. Some clans lost their kingship as quickly as it came as they were unable to present a male heir.

When the royal mantle fell on the Ubaka dynasty, it became clear that often, an heir was not produced until almost the end of the king's royal time stamp. Some perceived the Ubaka dynasty as blessed, while others perceived it as cursed, as no other child was ever born after the male child arrived.

Some members of the kingdom argued that it was better to have many children, regardless of the sex of the children, than to be stuck with a single male child. More children were a better option for the people of Ogbodo kingdom, since more children meant more hands helping to weed the farmlands.

In worse case scenarios, when the only child accidentally died, the parents became as miserable as they could be.

Thus, one can conclude that maybe the Ubaka dynasty might be cursed rather than blessed, after all.

Prince Obeze grew up learning the ways of kingship from an early age, as did his father. King Chigbo Ubaka wanted to ensure that his only son and child was well prepared for the great task ahead.

While there were no answers as to why the Ubaka dynasty always ended up with a male child towards the end of their royal term, Prince Obeze tried to remain positive and hope that things would be different for him.

Although things were not entirely different, as he too was in the same dilemma: already in his ninth year, and no heir to boast about.

Prince Obeze's union with Obiageli came shortly after his twenty-fifth birthday. Obiageli was the daughter of Ichie Agumba, the retired village principal. Ichie Agumba was the first man to shake the white man's hand when the missionaries visited the old elementary school in Ogbodo kingdom, which earned him his chieftaincy title of Ichie Agumba.

CHAPTER THREE

The deteriorating health of King Chigbo Ubaka was becoming a major concern in the kingdom. People were beginning to speculate, saying he may end up just like his father, King Udodi Ubaka the Great.

There were no visible signs of a mysterious ailment, but the king's health was questionable, and not even Ezemmuo, the chief priest, could save him.

Prince Obeze Ubaka was apprehensive because he knew that, soon, the mantle of leadership would fall on his shoulders.

His fear of failing his father and breaking the royal lineage, due to the absence of a male child, filled him with sadness. This sadness burdened Obeze's heart as he walked towards the royal palace.

He could hear the ikoro, summoned by the king, for the elders had gathered. People spoke in whispers, and only members of the king's royal cabinet were allowed inside the throne room.

The rest of the villagers stood outside the courtyard, awaiting an update on the king's health. Anytime the sound of the ikoro was heard, there must be something lurking. It meant that something was about to unfold or had progressed, either good news or bad.

The royal chamber was filled with council members and cabinet chiefs. The cabinet chiefs all had red caps with a feather attached to the left side corner. The chiefs commanded respect and were known to be noble men.

Ezemmuo announced his presence by stamping his staff of office on the ground as hard as he could. It rattled like a snake.

As Ezemmuo entered the room in his red robe with an old woven bag slung across his shoulders, he glanced at the people. Without saying a word, he walked vigorously into King Chigbo Ubaka's inner chambers. Everyone outside the king's inner chambers could hear Ezemmuo's incantations.

Queen Nnedi Ubaka carefully laid a cool damp cloth on the king's forehead to help reduce the fever.

Obeze held his father's hands while Obiageli helped Queen Nnedi fetch more water to wash the king, since he had not had a normal bath in days.

Ezemmuo placed some herbal mixtures on the king's chest and rubbed others on the king's face.

"That should help his breathing and subside the cough by the time he wakes up," Ezemmuo said. He moved swiftly around the room, uttering incantations in the form of musical chants.

Ezemmuo shook his head suddenly like he was possessed by a demon. In spiritual premonition, he moved back and forth after each chant of his incantations.

King Chigbo Ubaka's hands moved in a slow frenzy. Prince Obeze cried out as he stood up in a haste and stared at the king's motionless body.

Prince Obeze's face lit up in joyous anticipation that his father was about to wake up. King Ubaka pulled Obeze closer to his face. He smiled weakly at his wife, Nnedi, who by now was crying while holding onto her husband's weak hands. King Chigbo started coughing as he feebly wriggled his back against the bed. Ezemmuo leaned forward and applied oil, made with local spice, on the king's forehead.

"The throne is yours, my son. I am ready to join my ancestors," King Ubaka announced in a low tone as he continued coughing.

He fixed his gaze on Obeze. King Ubaka was very weak and pale and he groaned as he coughed; Obeze could tell he was in much pain.

"No, Father, you are not going to die!" Obeze replied in a shaky voice. He was scared, but he also knew the time was near for his father to join the spirits. King Ubaka grabbed Obeze's hands and placed them on his chest. He gave Nnedi a pat on the shoulders with a weak smile, then closed his eyes, breathing his last.

The women ran out of the room, crying and screaming. Ezemmuo approached the dead king's body and placed a leaf on the king's hands to depict the beginning of his journey into the spirit world.

Ezemmuo rolled out the white cloth underneath the king's bed and stretched it to cover King Ubaka's face.

Prince Obeze was speechless, as though a shockwave had taken over his thoughts. He stared at his father's lifeless body through teary eyes. Though his mouth was open, no words came out.

Ezemmuo left the king's inner chamber and walked calmly through the palace hallway to the throne room, where he notified the cabinet chiefs who were waiting patiently for confirmation of the sad news.

The sound of the ikoro stopped. Everyone could tell something bad had happened. Ezemmuo made his way to the courtyard where the people were gathered. By now, he was sure they already knew about the king's demise since the screaming of Queen Nnedi and Obiageli were loud enough to wake the dead. As the sound of the ikoro faded away in quick succession, Ezemmuo breathed heavily as he approached the courtyard.

"The king of Ogbodo kingdom, King Chigbo Ubaka, has joined his ancestors."

CHAPTER FOUR

Prince Obeze wandered endlessly in the forest of Umuokpo. The death of his father had put him in dire anguish. He needed time to be alone to clear his overwhelmed thoughts.

He did not realise how far into the forest he had wandered. Alone, he had all the time he needed to clear his head before ascending the throne as the new king of Ogbodo kingdom.

Prince Obeze pushed through leaves and branches as he walked aimlessly. Umuokpo was known for its abundance of wildlife species, something that attracted tourists from all over the neighbouring kingdoms.

As Prince Obeze approached the border between Umuokpo and Abaziani, he knew that he was not alone. He stopped unexpectedly to decipher the direction of the noise which made the leaves tremble.

Footsteps became louder and closer as though a person were approaching. At first, Prince Obeze thought it was a wild beast since he was touring their territories, and he needed to take every preventative measure not to be seen and eaten. He bent over to hide his presence.

"Show yourself or you die!" Obeze exclaimed from his hiding spot.

The footsteps stopped, and the leaves became still. At first the forest was silent as it could be, until, in a slow but steady rush, a voice said to Obeze, "I do not seek thee; I only seek my trap." The voice was feminine and only a short distance from Obeze's hiding spot.

"I am coming out now without a weapon. If you have yours, put it away in the name of the gods," the female voice said, making a hasty movement that stirred the shrubs.

"Why should I trust you?" Prince Obeze yelled.

"Well, you don't have to," the female voice lashed out in defense. The woman rushed forward.

She stood firmly with a fearless look, staring at Prince Obeze confidently. On her face, she wore shiny black mboko powder, a local cosmetic used by maidens to enhance their natural beauty.

Her breasts were well formed with tense pointed nipples tied gracefully inside an attractive printed wrapper. The beads around her waist dangled as she shook her hips vigorously.

Her legs were pleasingly dotted with local makeup, called nzu, which was typically mixed with charcoal to create a nice blend of colour.

Her hair was prettily woven as if she was getting ready to be married; the braids were held in place with thread from dried and processed sheep skin.

Obeze made a welcoming gesture as he walked carefully towards her, observing her countenance as he approached.

"What name do they call you, and what is a beautiful maiden doing in the forest all alone?" Obeze asked.

"Call me Nneoma! And for the records, you ask too many questions!" Nneoma arrogantly replied as she shook her hips enthusiastically, while holding her basket which carried her farm tools and hunting traps.

Obeze looked inside Nneoma's basket and could not help laughing. He wondered what the answer would be if he asked her another question.

"You farm and you hunt? Are you also a warrior?" Obeze asked sarcastically while avoiding her eyes.

The maidens of Umuokpo and Abaziani were known to be very strong. Whatever the men could do, the women could do better. It was known that the men were lazy, since the women were strong enough to do any kinds of jobs, such as farming and hunting.

Obeze admired the strength of Nneoma, as such a skill set was not typical in Ogbodo kingdom. There, the women were child-bearing tools, while the men were responsible for providing for the family, doing all the farm work, and hunting down meat for the steaming pot of soup.

"I farm and I hunt, and I can fight if necessary," Nneoma replied agitatedly, as she searched the bushes for her traps. "What are you doing here anyway; are you a hunter? You are not from this village either." Nneoma grinned at Obeze.

"Now you ask too many questions," Obeze said with a smile. "I am not a hunter, but I can shoot down an animal if necessary; well, maybe, if I was starving to death." He laughed, and so did Nneoma.

Obeze continued, "Let me help you with that." He gently grabbed the deer's head, while Nneoma released the trap that had caught it.

As he bent over to help, Nneoma's hands brushed against his as he tried to pull the deer out of the clamp. Her well rounded buttocks pushed forward, revealing her waist curves. Obeze could feel her breadth as her hands caressed his gently.

"Thanks for your help," Nneoma said, as she cleaned her hands with dry leaves. "You are not from Abaziani?" She used a hunting knife to expertly butcher the deer, and then placed the pieces inside her basket and covered them with leaves.

"I am from Ogbodo community." Obeze hesitated as he did not want to reveal his identity. No one knew he was there in the forest, and he wanted to keep it that way.

"Oh! That kingdom with a dead king?" Nneoma said nonchalantly. "That must be very hard for the queen and the prince." Nneoma sounded compassionate.

"It is indeed a difficult time," Obeze replied as he leaned his back against a tree. He began to feel agitated as the thought of his father's death came rushing back into his mind. His time with Nneoma had seemed, until now, to be a good distraction.

"Are you alright?" Nneoma asked, staring at Obeze as though she was trying to piece together his thoughts.

"What do they call you?" Nneoma asked with a depreciating grin.

Obeze slid his back gently down the tree until he reached the ground.

He buried his head in between his arms. Nneoma gently put her basket down, leaned towards Obeze, and grabbed his arm. She pushed her upper body against his as he held up his face.

Obeze sniffed to clear his sobs. He did not want to appear weak in the presence of a strange beautiful maiden. With his vulnerable state of mind, he knew he was not in control of his emotions anymore.

Nneoma cuddled Obeze like a mother would hold on to a crying child. She was not sure why the strange man was feeling sad. She pressed her body against his as they both lay on the ground under the guava tree.

"I am just a man with a troubled heart," Obeze said as he caressed Nneoma's face. "I came here to find solitude and peace! That is all you need to know about me." Obeze shut his eyes to stop the tears from tickling down.

As handsome as Prince Obeze was, it was difficult for a maiden to resist his looks.

Obeze and Nneoma locked gazes as Nneoma allowed him to touch her in a manner that made her whine.

She welcomed his hands as they quickly moved all over her body. The heat and passion were intense as she began to sweat profusely. Each of Obeze's touches sent shivering vibes throughout her body.

They moaned as they succumbed to the heat of passion, with each thrust sending a feeling of serenity into Prince Obeze.

Having desecrated his body with Nneoma, allowing his vulnerability to get in the way of his right judgment, Obeze bound Nneoma to secrecy to never speak of their act to anyone.

CHAPTER FIVE

It had been seven market days since the death and funeral of King Chigbo Ubaka. Obeze would be crowned king in the next eke market day.

The funeral of the late king kept everyone talking in awe. All the traditional rulers from the neighbouring communities were present at the ceremony. Different dance groups of all ages were present as well.

The masquerade display was phenomenal. Masquerade was a sacred cult fully dominated by men. Women were banned from seeing masquerades and would hide beneath tall trees to watch the performances, while the men gallantly danced around the masquerade with bottles of dry gin.

The funeral ceremony lasted for seven days. On each day, a different phase of the ritual rites of passage were performed by Ezemmuo and all the other chief priests and priestesses from different communities.

All the rituals were to grant the late king an easy and quick passage to the ancestral world. As soon as the king was buried, there began an ancestral dance by all the chief priests representing the entire deities of the seven clans.

Shortly after the king's funeral, the coronation plans began for Prince Obeze. It was sacrilege for the throne to be vacant for too long.

Even though Prince Obeze had not yet produced a male heir, the late King Chigbo Ubaka had Prince Obeze take over from him. He had believed until the end of his life that Prince Obeze would make a strong, wise ruler and would very soon produce an heir.

Obeze's coronation was very flamboyant. Obiageli was adorned with beautiful body beads and makeup. She was well kilted in a tightly woven, damask fabric, well tied around her chest.

Obeze was dressed in a glowing, flowing gown, and beautifully adorned with beads around his neck and wrists. He held an elephant tusk in his left hand, and ofor in his right hand.

The ofor was the symbol of kingship and leadership. Ezemmuo did his usual incantations and spiritual dance before placing the crown on Obeze's head.

The king's cabinet chiefs and other traditional rulers were present to witness the great ceremony.

With the ritual complete, Ezemmuo presented the new king to the people.

"People of Ogbodo kingdom, friends and well-wishers of the people of Ogbodo! Here is your new king! King Obeze Ubaka of Ogbodo kingdom!" Ezemmuo yelled in a compelling voice.

The people responded, "Long live our king! Long live our king!"

King Obeze shook his head in agreement to the chant.

"Well done, my people; may the gods of our land keep and preserve us all."

The people responded in a chorus: "Ise," meaning Amen.

By three months after the coronation, King Obeze was getting used to his new status as king of Ogbodo kingdom. But his heart remained troubled over his childlessness dilemma. He was afraid that members of other clans might begin to nurture rebellion and take the throne from him by force. They would have the force of tradition on their side.

Obeze also suffered from guilt, which had no mercy on him, as he could not get his mind off of his sacrilegious act with Nneoma, an act done in the heat of uncontrollable passion, instigated by his vulnerable emotions at the time.

King Obeze could not stop blaming himself for giving up his self-control.

He knew he had failed Obiageli by defiling his body without her consent.

While it didn't appear wrong to bed another woman according to the traditions, as men were allowed to marry as many women as they could, even if Obeze wanted Nneoma, he couldn't have her as his wife since she was not a native of Ogbodo.

Events were beginning to look complicated for King Obeze and Queen Obiageli. If no heir were announced in the next nine months, the kingship would have to leave the Ubaka dynasty.

The presence of Obiageli went unnoticed, as King Obeze drowned himself in thoughts of childlessness, guilt, and anguish.

"My lord, why do you look troubled?" Queen Obiageli broke

into Obeze's thoughts as he raised his brows in surprise.

"Oh, my queen, I didn't see or hear you approach," Obeze explained as he held unto Obiageli's hands.

"I was just thinking of my father, the late king," Obeze lied as he looked away to avoid Obiageli's eyes.

"May the gods of our land welcome his spirit," Obiageli said.

"My lord, it is past midnight and I want you by my side in bed," Obiageli said calmly as she stroked Obeze's chin with her hands.

"My queen, sleep eludes me, and my heart aches with thoughts!"

"Nevertheless, that is not enough reason to stay in denial of your succulent breasts. I shall join you shortly," Obeze said with a wide grin.

Obiageli smiled as though she had been tickled, and she brushed her feet against the mat as she made her way into her chambers.

King Obeze smiled as he watched Obiageli exit; her hips shook forcefully enough to arouse a sleeping man.

The night was so quiet and peaceful, one could see the stars in the thickness of the dark clouds. Obeze allowed the humid wind to slap his face as he reached the balcony, heading towards his chambers.

He did not want to keep his wife waiting, although he first needed to clear his mind from disturbing thoughts. He needed reassurance from the gods, and answers to his questions.

King Obeze knew that, whatever the case may be, when there is a will, there will surely be a way. He closed the balcony door, locked the doors to the royal chambers, and retired for the night.

CHAPTER SIX

As morning approached, King Obeze was awoken by what sounded like sobs. Obiageli was crying.

"My queen, what troubles your heart at this early hour?" King Obeze felt astonished and scared as he searched Obiageli's face for answers.

"Time is running out, my lord!" Obiageli moaned as she sat up from the bed, pushing her back against the headboard. "If nothing is done soon, the Ubaka dynasty will be gone forever! I will be selfish and filled with guilt to deny you an heir! Maybe it's time you married another wife!"

Obiageli drew out those last words with caution as she knew they may anger King Obeze. The last time the mention of another bride came up, the king was furious. He loved Obiageli and did not want to put her through that dilemma of sharing a husband with another woman.

"And what is the guarantee that the new bride would bear a child?" King Obeze asked in a rather annoyed tone. He tried not to show off that flare of anger that was already building up.

"You know how I feel each time we have these conversations about childlessness! I cannot question the gods, but getting another bride is not an option!" King Obeze said angrily.

"What other options are out there?" Obeze asked as he stared at Queen Obiageli. The queen was still drenched in her sobs, and she sniffed as she wiped her face with the back of her hands.

Obiageli looked up into the domed ceiling of the king's royal chambers. She turned and stared at Obeze like someone about to confess to a deadly crime.

"I have an idea," Obiageli said in a rather nervous voice. "We can falsify my pregnancy. Then on the ninth month, we can arrange for a baby from a neighbouring village such as Abaziani or Umuokpo. There is an orphanage in Abaziani being managed by a midwife. We can arrange for a male child. We shall present the child to the people as the heir to the throne after your reign. This will secure the throne to remain with the Ubaka dynasty." Queen

Obiageli finished off her speech as she clutched the pillow tightly.

King Obeze sat up at the corner of the bed with the feeling of a death sentence. Astonishingly surprised by his wife's suggestion, he understood it to be the plan of a desperate woman. Adopting a son was not a bad idea but lying to the people made him bitter.

King Obeze did not want to lose the throne, as an adopted child would not be eligible to be king since the child was not a product of his sperm. The tradition clearly forbade that. However, desperate times required desperate measures.

King Obeze was perplexed with a feeling of excitement and confusion.

"My queen, what possesses you at this hour of the morning to think of such thoughts?" Obeze asked with a look of incomprehension. "I hope you have not mentioned this to anyone." Obeze gave Obiageli a stern look.

"My lord, no one knows about this. These thoughts remain with us alone," Obiageli said reassuringly.

King Obeze was overwhelmed with the risky solution to their impending problem. Obiageli waited patiently on King Obeze's decision to the plan, which was the best she could come up with.

The silence in the room felt very uncomfortable to Obiageli. Obeze had not said much since Obiageli fed him her gruesome plan of lies and deceit.

While it was King Obeze's desire to have an heir that would secure the throne, he did not want to jeopardise the family's name and the oath he took to uphold the truth, peace, and security of the kingdom.

Moreover, how could he deny his wife the joy of being called "mother," since the act of childlessness could be his fault. If it were a curse, only the gods could decide when to remove it.

Finally, Obeze said, "If we do this, the midwife of Abaziani would have to swear with her life that none of this become known to anyone. If this ever becomes known, let the gods take my life in appeasement for the land and the people of Ogbodo kingdom. I have spoken." King Obeze concluded with the feeling of right judgement.

Obiageli reached out to King Obeze in a warm embrace. She pressed her body against his as she knelt before him, grabbing his two hands. "All shall be well," Queen Obiageli said with a kiss on the king's lips.

"The feast of the new yam festival is fast approaching, and I will make the announcement of your conception," King Obeze said as he squeezed Obiageli's hands softly.

"Thank you, my lord; may your days be long," Queen Obiageli whispered.

CHAPTER SEVEN

The feast of the new yam festival was always a celebration long awaited; everyone looked forward to it.

It was a time when the men got drunk on palm wine. It was also Ugboko's favorite time of the year.

Ugboko was the village drunk, who would stagger from one place to another, drenched in the smell of alcohol.

Ugboko's whole family was known for drunkenness. Some people said it ran in their blood.

His father, Iweji, was known as the village clown, as he always made children laugh. Women feared him, as he would continuously chase them around with sticks.

Iweji could crack jokes from morning to evening while gulping down bottles of freshly brewed palm wine.

Each time kids saw Ugboko, they would make a big circle on the ground with a stick and invite Ugboko inside the circle. They would throw pebbles at him while singing a song to catch his attention.

The feast of the new yam festival was also a ceremony that attracted clans and people from all other villages and communities. It was also a prosperous period for the maidens, as most of them ended up getting married or getting pregnant without being married, whichever one came first.

During the new yam festival, the people thanked the gods for a good harvest while they ushered in the new yams and prayed for more blessings from the gods. It was usually held after the harvest season began. No one could eat the new yams until the ceremony had taken place.

However, the festival was also a time when masquerade performers showed off their new costumes and exotic dance displays.

King Obeze enjoyed the masquerade performances; he had always wanted to be part of the masquerade cult but that was prohibited due to his royal bloodline.

King Obeze reflected on his childhood experiences and the beliefs about masquerade that he was told to trust. He chuckled as those memories came flooding back. His father, the late King Chigbo, once told him that masquerades were the dead ancestors sent back to life with a message for the living. Moreover, they were divine messengers of the gods.

King Obeze was amused by how many of these stories one had to put up with as a kid.

As he prepared for the big day, he became burdened with mixed feelings of fear and excitement as this was going to be his first new yam festival as the king of Ogbodo kingdom.

It was the morning of the new yam festival; the palace was nicely decorated. The maiden servants washed clean the entire rooms in the palace vigorously. The barn was cleared out of old yams in preparation for the intake of the new yams.

The maidens adorned themselves with beautiful beads as they prepared for the maiden dance, while the masquerade cult was getting ready for their intoxicating dance display.

Ezemmuo came in and sanctified the arena and offered sacrifices to the gods of fertile lands and harvest. The first set of yams to be dug out would be given to the women to cook with fresh palm oil which would be brought out to the arena.

King Obeze and Queen Obiageli made their way to the arena nicely dressed in fine prints. The people chanted the king's praise as he made his entrance and geared up for his big speech.

"My people, you are all welcome to this great feast of the new yam festival," King Obeze spoke as he raised his ofor, the symbol of kingship.

"This has been a long-standing tradition by our fathers and forefathers, and we live today because we are custodians of these rites and traditions! As the king of this great kingdom, I declare the ceremony open."

Loud thunderous roars and shouts came flying from the jubilant crowd.

The maiden dance quickly took over the arena as the maidens shook their hips vigorously to the tune of the local drums. The masquerade dance commenced as soon as the maiden dance was over. The people were thrilled, and everyone danced joyously.

As soon as the yam was cooked, the women presented it to the king.

"My people! Here is the new yam," King Obeze said as he raised his hands up for everyone to see the yam. "Here is the reason we are all gathered here today. May our ancestors receive our offering of this bountiful harvest." King Obeze invited other kings and traditional rulers to eat with him.

King Obeze took a piece of yam, dipped it in the palm oil, and ate it with a nod. Other kings joined in devouring the yam.

Ezemmuo approached the arena, picked up a piece of yam and, with his face raised, chanted, "May we eat and never lack or go hungry; may our lives be enriched by the gift of this new yam for many years to come"

"Iseeeeeeeeee," the people reaffirmed.

The ceremony went on with singing, dancing, eating, and cultural displays from other clans and communities.

King Obeze summoned the people together after they had had a fair share of yam with palm oil. The women cooked more yams and brought them out to the arena, so everyone had enough to eat. The king and the cabinet chiefs gathered.

The crowd was summoned to keep quiet, everyone staring at each other while waiting for King Obeze to speak.

"My people, the great people of Ogbodo kingdom, I have great news! The gods have finally spoken! Obiageli my wife, your queen, is with child."

King Obeze breathed heavily as the silence in the arena quickly turned into praise, songs, and jubilation.

Queen Obiageli smiled at King Obeze as soon as he made the announcement. She caressed her stomach gently as a gesture of a child growing in it.

The women all danced around the queen, offering prayers and thanking the gods for the gift of a child. Queen

Obiageli joined the women in the dance as the crowd cheered.

The cabinet chiefs began to greet the king with three handshakes, using the back of their palms. Noble men were known to greet one another in that manner.

Once again, the people chanted, "May the gods be praised."

The evening was filled with talk about the announcement of the new child and the that hope it brought to the Ubaka royal family, since the child was long overdue and had been waited on for almost ten years.

CHAPTER EIGHT

Living with the guilt of the only option to keep the royal lineage going, King Obeze could not get over the announcement of Obiageli's conception plot.

He wondered if he had made the right decision in supporting his wife's plan. Nothing was more exciting than the cry of a baby around the palace, but he imagined he may have gone about it the wrong way.

Still, going the right way would cost him the throne as an adopted child would never be allowed to be king. All these thoughts rampaged through the mind of King Obeze.

As he paced his inner chamber, he smiled at the memories of the previous day's yam festival and how well it went. It was a long-awaited festival of the people and celebrating it with the people as their king was indeed a blessing.

In his thoughtful mood, King Obeze reflected upon his life as a young child and heir. He imagined what life would be like for the child that would be given to them as an heir apparent.

His life as a young prince was a life of guards and palace helpers. A life that gave up all privileges of being a normal kid. A life that had him sneak out on several occasions to go rabbit hunting with his peers, and breaking palm kernels with stone and sucking out the juice.

Sometimes they would fly kites and watch a kite get trapped in Maazi Ogbuji's plantation. He owned so many plantations and palm wine gardens that all grew as tall as ebube-ututu, the walking stick masquerade that comes out once every five years.

Maazi Ogbuji's lands, trees, and plantations were home to lots of damaged kites that flew up and never made it down. Maazi Ogbuji died, leaving his lands to his three sons who sold most of the lands and relocated to the white man's country.

How times have changed! King Obeze chuckled at his satisfying thoughts. Back in those days, it was forbidden to sell lands handed down to you by your father.

The lands were sacred and meant to remain in the family. In recent times, nothing seemed to be an abomination anymore. Sons sold lands and moved far away from home and sometimes never came back.

King Obeze paced even more as his thoughts took him down memory lane. Having lost much of his childhood, his adulthood was now filled with fear and uncertainty. A fear he must face alone, without the guidance of a father.

"How long have you been standing there?" King Obeze asked as he turned around and saw Queen Obiageli at the entrance of his chamber.

"Long enough to know that my husband has immersed himself in thoughts," Obiageli responded, as she walked past the old lamp sitting on the bedside table.

"I didn't hear the door open," King Obeze replied, mystified.

"The door was unlocked, so I let myself in," Queen Obiageli explained.

She knew her husband was going through several emotional moments. King Obeze still had not gotten over the death of his father, and now the decision to adopt a child was indeed heavy.

Obiageli was a bit reluctant to speak to Obeze, not sure if it was the right time. She did not like breaking into his thoughts.

Sometimes King Obeze would be petulant if his thoughts were interrupted and this moment appeared to be one of those times.

"My husband, I know this may not be a good time to talk to you, but we need to talk," Obiageli said cautiously while trying to gauge Obeze's expression.

"Speak, my ear listens," King Obeze responded.

"I sent for the midwife of Abaziani. She arrived and I have an update to share with you." Obiageli stopped talking, as she was unsure whether Obeze was listening to what she had to say.

"What news do you carry?" King Obeze asked.

"I met with Nnejekwu last night; she is the midwife in charge of the orphanage at Abaziani. She has been sworn to secrecy as we agreed."

Queen Obiageli cast a glance at King Obeze as she continued talking. "All the women in Ogbodo kingdom actually go to her during the time of birth, as that is the only orphanage servicing Umuokpo, Abaziani, and Ogbodo.

"She also confirmed that a certain maiden was expecting a male child which she plans to give up at birth." Obiageli bit her lips slightly as she settled into the chair beside the king's bed.

"What makes Nnejekwu so sure that the maiden would give up the baby?" Obeze asked, feeling slightly uncomfortable. Obiageli walked briskly towards King Obeze who was by now searching through his thoughts.

"My lord, Nnejekwu confirmed that the maiden confided in her that she didn't want the baby. No man would marry a woman who already has a child from another man. It was her intention to be married someday, however, the maiden is not sure who the father of the child was."

"A whore! A child of a whore?" King Obeze screamed as he stared at his wife agitatedly.

Obiageli knew she had to sound convincing; moreover, there was no turning back now, for the announcement of a coming heir had been made. The people were expectant.

Neither King Obeze nor Queen Obiageli wanted to raise suspicion amongst the people.

"What does it matter if it is a child of a whore?" Queen Obiageli snapped.

King Obeze paced the room with quick steps, breathing heavily, his mind vexed and angered. He knew he needed to decide with a clear mind.

In irritation, he said, "I hope we get this right! Things cannot go wrong! I am doing this because of the love I have for you, my queen. If this goes wrong in any way, I will take my life!"

CHAPTER NINE

As days rolled into weeks and months, Queen Obiageli's stomach grew like a melon from the safe potion that was secretly made for her by Nnejekwu. In the early months, Queen Obiageli tried hard to stage the morning sickness that comes with pregnancy.

The palace was in great anticipation of the birth of the new child. Nnejekwu always came to the palace to administer ante-natal care to the mother to be. Sacrifices were made in thankful appreciation to the god of fertility and conception, for the gift of a royal child.

The news excited King Obeze but scared him even more.

Nevertheless, the king's cabinet chiefs and Ezemmuo paid a visit to Ogbakiri, the god of births, to ensure that the queen gave birth safely.

Ogbakiri was regularly appeased with kolanuts, palm wine, yams, and a white peacock. Ogbakiri was known to be a very powerful god. It was believed that those women who either miscarried or had still births had unfinished scores to settle with that great deity.

Many women who were pregnant or seeking children ensured that the deity was well fed with sacrifices in return for a safe birth and a fertile womb.

Ogbakiri was known to be a sensitive deity. One needed to tread with caution when dealing with Ogbakiri. Any woman that had either aborted a child or carried the child of another man in marriage without the consent of her husband usually ended up with a miscarriage or a still birth.

During recent years, with the coming of the white man, it was now known that still births and miscarriages could be caused by underlying health issues, not necessarily by infidelity or abortions. Although to the present day, many people still hold onto this belief.

Nnejekwu was the only one allowed to care for Queen Obiageli. The palace maidens and guards were only allowed to see her or attend to her needs after Nnejekwu had taken proper precautions and cared for the queen.

Nnejekwu was known as the best midwife Umuokpo, Abaziani, and Ogbodo had ever had. Women from neighbouring villages traveled from far and wide to see her. Her love for children inspired her to open an orphanage where she cared mostly for unwanted or abandoned children, or children whose mothers had died at birth.

Nnejekwu received help from all neighbouring communities who donated baby items, food, and money towards the orphanage.

Everyone talked about the coming of the royal child. The child was coming just in time before the end of the ten-year royal shift. With a few months to go for Obiageli, every contingent plan had been put to place. The maiden carrying the adopted child should be due for delivery soon. Other women showed up at the palace with gifts for the mother-to-be. They danced and showered prayers on Obiageli as a sign of goodwill.

There was plenty of food and drinks as the kingdom was thrown into a festive mode in anticipation of the birth of the child.

There was more to come as soon as the child was born. Once the royal child arrived, the sound of the ikoro would be heard in all the nearby villages, after which Ezemmuo would offer a sacrifice of thanks to Ogbakiri for a fruitful birth.

The king's cabinet would then assemble at the palace to bless whatever name the king had chosen. The name of the child would then be taken to the great shrine of Ogbodo kingdom for a proclamation of destiny for the child.

King Obeze looked forward to the sound of the ikoro. The last time it was heard was during the death of King Chigbo Ubaka.

This time, the sound of the ikoro would bring respect and dignity to his throne. When the child would come, the sound of the ikoro will solidify his reign and bring to his lineage a continuous inheritance.

King Obeze wondered what life would be like for him when the child arrived. He was not sure if he was ready to be a father to an adopted son. He was not sure if he could love him the way a father would truly love a son.

He wondered if he would be a great dad just like his father was to him. His desire was to raise the boy as a prince that he would be, but he wished for a better circumstance associated with the coming of the child. A child he could call his own! A child that would call him father!

The queen would no longer be laughed at or called barren. King Obeze allowed his thoughts to run wild again as he retired to his chambers after a day of celebrating, offering sacrifices, and appeasing the gods. He quickly checked in on Obiageli who already retired to her chambers after a hectic day.

The ijeana festival, the festival of lands, was around the corner; something to distract King Obeze's thoughts before the child arrived.

As he entered his chambers, he carefully removed his crown and placed it on his bed side table. He made his way to his bed and drowned himself in sleep.

CHAPTER TEN

The ijeana festival, or festival of lands, was to celebrate any man with an abundance of land, either through inheritance or by virtue of affluence. Such men were considered blessed by their chi, or life force.

The festival of lands made it possible for the people to come together to celebrate and to offer sacrifices of thanks to their chi. It was usually celebrated once every three years.

It was also a time when men showed off the number of lands and the amount of wealth that they had.

Most of the maidens would wish for a man that had many lands to his name. The lands were a guarantee that the man could take care of his bride and children. Therefore, many fathers would willingly give away their daughters in marriage based on that assurance.

The people of Ogbodo kingdom looked forward to the festival. Most of all, the widows, the farmers who did not have lands of their own to farm, and anyone less privileged benefitted a lot from the festival. Some of them were given land by landowners as a gesture to give back to the community.

The festival had traditional rulers gracing the event, masquerade performances, women, and maiden cultural dance performances. Ezemmuo would perform the necessary rituals, while King Obeze opened the festival with a speech and a warm welcome to the guests.

The king's cabinet members were always present, all dressed in white flowing shirts and wrappers, and adorned with the red cap made for titled men.

After the maidens had exhausted their strength in dance, Ezemmuo took over the arena, dancing around the courtyard, walking in circles with his enchanting melodic rhythms.

Ezemmuo called upon all the landowners, summoning them to kneel in his presence. He then offered prayers to the gods as he laid a tiny, brown clay pot on the head of each man in the circle.

Each of the men handed over the pot to another. When the pot came to the last man kneeling, Ezemmuo took it and placed it carefully on the ground.

After the entire ritual was over, the festival continued with the masquerade dance performance.

King Obeze was excited but overwhelmed with the ceremony. He was overwhelmed as the time was drawing near for his wife to travel to Abaziani with Nnejekwu to bring home their child.

Arrangements had been made for that trip, but King Obeze was drenched with worry as to the outcome of the arrangement.

The king imagined the betrayal that would emerge from this, should the plan fail or become known. His thoughts caused him anguish, but he knew that any show of weakness would be detrimental to their plan.

They had come this far to protect what rightfully belonged to his family: his lineage.

King Obeze prayed silently to the gods to keep his secrets and to protect the unborn child that would soon become prince and heir apparent of Ogbodo kingdom. Only one thing awaited.

The sound of the ikoro! The birth of the child awaited a few more market days.

CHAPTER ELEVEN

The queen had been gone for almost a week now. King Obeze was troubled as there had been no news of childbirth yet. He walked through the courtyard with a cup of palm wine to help calm his nerves.

He could not get his mind off the child and his wife. What if the baby is dead? Or, what if the maiden refused to let go of the baby?

These horrific thoughts played in the king's mind. He wandered blindly as he tried to get his mind off those insane imaginations.

It was the first day of the eke market day. The sun was out, and the air was humid but felt satisfying. The birds were cooing to the rhythm of the muggy wind. Women were chattering with baskets on their heads on their ways to the market.

The men would usually hold onto a tote of palm wine and dry gin to open the stomach in anticipation of the delicacies that would be served later in the day.

There was hardly a household in Ogbodo kingdom that did not have at least a keg of palm wine stacked away somewhere in the corner of the house. It was an essential drink, just like water, and was mainly used to welcome guests. The eke market day was the busiest one in Ogbodo kingdom. Men, women, and children took part in the trade of farm produce to the neighbouring communities.

While the market was at its peak, many travellers stopped over for meals and supplies. Most of the travellers came from Abaziani, especially families with loved ones at the orphanage or wives at the birthing room within the walls of the orphanage.

Abaziani was known to be blessed with great natural herbal medicine.

Men and women of Abaziani were also known to be warriors, farmers, and hunters. The eke market day in Ogbodo kingdom was known to be the largest of its kind as the people benefitted from the revenue the market generated.

Similarly, the people of Abaziani benefitted from the revenue their health facilities provided. The two communities worked together and enjoyed that which they had in common.

Men from Abaziani came to Ogbodo kingdom to marry. There was a saying that goes like this: "Marry an Abaziani woman and you will be unable to tell who the breadwinner of the family is."

That saying scared the men of Abaziani, as they feared their wives would become warriors and hunters and challenge their male ego.

While women became farmers, warriors, and hunters in Abaziani, the men of Abaziani were known to be lazy and unproductive, only useful in the act of procreation.

The maidens of Ogbodo kingdom would gladly refuse marriage with a native of Abaziani because none of them wanted a lazy man for a husband.

King Obeze waited patiently for news to emerge from Abaziani regarding Queen Obiageli and the child. In as much as he knew that his wife was not actually pregnant, he prayed for her safety and that of the unborn child.

King Obeze sat in his throne room. He exhaled and murmured as he made utterances to himself. He reached out to the keg of palm wine, but as he shook it, he knew that was going to be the last cup.

Every morning the guards would ensure that fresh palm wine was in the keg and dropped off in the throne room. The guards would drink from it first to ensure it was safe for consumption.

Dusk had approached, and still no news came from Abaziani. King Obeze had already sent word to the cabinet chiefs to gather in his throne room. He had also sent emissaries to Abaziani to oversee the affair there and to ensure that all was well with his wife.

King Obeze wished he could be in Abaziani with Queen Obiageli, but the king was not allowed to leave the palace on such quest, as a man had no business with birthing matters.

The cabinet chiefs arrived at the palace, perturbed as to why the king had summoned them at that time of the day. Meetings were never held at nighttime except in an emergency.

King Obeze was getting ready to break the silence in the room when Maazi Ibekwe stormed in as if he were being chased by a lion. Maazi Ibekwe was one of the emissaries sent to Abaziani.

"My king! I have news! Your wife, our queen, has brought forth a male child!"

In excitement, King Obeze stood up from his seat and ran to the window; he searched aimlessly into the dark!

"Where are the guards? Guards! Guards! Summon them here and initiate the sound of the ikoro! Indeed, something great has happened! My royal cabinet, a prince is born unto us this day!" King Obeze screamed, his footsteps slapping the marble tiles.

The cabinet chiefs were all excited about the news and started talking in loud whispers.

Ebuka, the palace guard, ran as fast as he could and joined the cabinet chiefs.

"My king, I hear it!" cried Maazi Ibekwe. "I hear the sound of the ikoro!"

Although it sounded faint and distant, as the sound drew closer and became louder, a grin lit up Obeze's face.

"An heir, a baby prince!" King Obeze kept chanting, as the cabinet chiefs all stood up, each speaking loudly and uttering prayers of thanksgiving.

The room was filled with chattering. People began to gather in the king's courtyard as the sound of the ikoro was audible enough to wake a sleeping child.

King Obeze, accompanied by the cabinet chiefs and Ezemmuo, quickly walked out of the throne room to the courtyard to welcome and address the people.

"My people, today the Ubaka dynasty welcome the birth of the prince! Your queen, my wife, has brought to life a baby boy!"

"A prince! And an heir apparent!" The crowd cheered with uncontrollable joy.

"As we await the homecoming of the child alongside his mother, we thank the gods for a continuous reign of the Ubaka dynasty," King Obeze continued his speech, as the people listened in utter tranquility.

"As the king of Ogbodo kingdom, I, King Obeze Ubaka, decree that my son, the heir apparent to the throne of Ogbodo kingdom, shall be called Sọchima!"

The people cheered for him again.

"Our king has spoken, and so shall it be!" Ezemmuo exclaimed.

CHAPTER TWELVE

Finally, Queen Obiageli returned to the palace with the baby, Sọchima Ubaka, accompanied by Nnejekwu the midwife. Endless strings of guests flooded inside the palace to pay homage to the baby.

King Obeze presented the child to the people, while Queen Obiageli rested from the long trip from Abaziani all the way back to Ogbodo kingdom.

The men drank countless rounds of palm wine while breaking kola nuts. They filled the entire room with roars of laughter.

Ebuka was now the palace guard, the son of Obika the chief guard, who served the late king Chigbo Ubaka during his reign. Ebuka ensured the palm wine kegs were replenished with fresh ones as the men continued to empty the kegs.

Queen Obiageli was presented with a special meal from the women of Ogbodo kingdom. It was of boiled yam with fresh fish soup, and it was a special meal given to every woman who gave birth to a child. The herbal spices in the fish soup helped the womb heal faster.

As the evening approached, things became quieter in the palace. The guests were beginning to disperse. King Obeze made his way to his chambers.

As he walked across the hall, he could not help the tingles of excitement that he felt. King Obeze was happy to be called a father, a king with an heir apparent. Although he was not biologically connected to the child, they seemed to share the special bond that could be expected between a father and a son.

King Obeze imagined Sọchima all grown up and ready to learn the ways of kingship. He thought about what life had in store for the young child.

Just before he made the final walk to his chambers, King Obeze stopped in the throne room where Ebuka was keeping watch.

"Ebuka!" King Obeze called out.

"Yes, my king." Ebuka rushed over and knelt before King Obeze.

"I request the presence of Nnejekwu. I believe she is in the queen's chambers. Bring her to my private chambers," King Obeze said. Ebuka stood up and ran to the queen's private chambers.

As Nnejekwu stood before king Obeze, she could not help but detect the excitement in the king's grin, but also the fear in his eyes.

King Obeze paced his private meeting room enclosed within the walls of his inner chambers. Nnejekwu was feeling anxious in the king's presence, as she was unsure of the reason for the call.

"Nnejekwu, I want to thank you for what you have done for my family." King Obeze broke the silence in the room.

"Thank you, my king, may your reign be long," Nnejekwu replied in a steady voice.

"We both know the story behind the birth of Sọchima. I want to remind you that we are all bound by oath to keep it away from everyone," King Obeze said with a stern look.

Nnejekwu knelt before King Obeze.

"Yes, my king, I have sworn to say nothing to anyone."

Nnejekwu stood up and sat on the chair, her face drenched in perspiration which she wiped with her wrapper.

"Tell me, what happened to the whore who bore this child?" King Obeze asked arrogantly as he threw a quick glance at Nnejekwu.

"My king, she is not a whore, but a maiden from Umuokpo. I do not know a lot about her. I only know she was to be married to a man from Abaziani.

"She came to me pregnant and she did not know who was responsible.

The maiden told me that she had been raped, and that, since the incident happened, the man from Abaziani refused to continue with the marriage rites.

"She gave birth to the boy and vanished from the orphanage. My king, she has gone in search of a new life in another community. She made it clear she did not want anything to do with the child of a stranger whom had done her such harm. She said the child was a curse to her."

Nnejekwu ended her sermon, trying to look and sound convincing, as King Obeze stared at her with doubt in his eyes.

"My king, you have nothing to worry about. I have been in this orphanage for twenty-nine years, and I have seen many women come and go. Such types never come back."

Nnejekwu was trying to make King Obeze feel comfortable.

"What if all she told you was a lie?" King Obeze asked rhetorically, trying to justify his doubts.

"My king, I assure you, there is nothing to worry about," Nnejekwu said in a soothing tone. "I understand your concerns, but everything was properly put in place. The maiden in question will not be coming back! They never come back! Remember, she is already an outcast. Remember the tradition that states any maiden that carries the child of a man that is not her husband will be banished as an outcast?"

"But the child!? The child of an outcast is indeed a cursed child!" King Obeze affirmed.

"No, my king! He is not!" Nnejekwu argued. "The child is innocent and has his own destiny to live up to. His destiny has nothing to do with the choices his mother has made."

King Obeze smiled as he inhaled deeply. He knew Nnejekwu was right. Passing judgement on an innocent child because of his mother's choices was a wrong thing to do.

Now this child belonged to him, would live in his palace, would call him father someday, and finally would become king. A child that was led to him by fate.

"Thank you, Nnejekwu, you have indeed made my days longer! As king of Ogbodo kingdom, I will ensure you are richly rewarded." King Obeze smiled at Nnejekwu.

"Thank you, my king; may your days be long."

CHAPTER THIRTEEN

In the next nineteen years, Sọchima grew to be a fine young man, a fierce warrior and hunter, not typical of an Ogbodo youth. He was handsome and strong, and fearless yet humble.

As a prince, he was not expected to farm or hunt, but he loved setting traps around the palace courtyard to catch bush meat. He also loved weeding and planting in the palace garden.

Obiageli's love for Sọchima knew no bounds. She adored Sọchima. He was a child with so many skills and talents, and he was more typical of an Umuokpo or Abaziani bloodline. He would challenge warriors from

Abaziani and Umuokpo to a fight, and his skills were exceptional.

He taught the palace guards how to catch bush meat, and he taught the palace maidens how to harvest cassava. It was impossible not to love him, and everyone did.

Amongst the palace maidens was a beautiful young woman from Abaziani serving as the palace steward. She was tall, slim, well endowed with a nicely curved waist, and she had well-rounded hips that could stir up a man's desires. Her thick dark hair hung below her shoulders. She was called Erimma.

Sọchima loved Erimma. She was gentle, caring, and loved to be around Sọchima always. She loved to hunt and would also challenge Sọchima to a friendly fight. She came to the palace as a child and grew up with Sọchima.

King Obeze was very uncomfortable with the relationship that was beginning to grow between Sọchima and Erimma, which he feared might grow deeper if not curbed.

According to the traditions, an heir apparent was not allowed to marry from another kingdom. Sọchima must pick a bride from Ogbodo kingdom.

King Obeze thought it may be a good time to start teaching Sọchima the duties of a future king. King Obeze mused on how fast the years had gone by.

The king could remember Sọchima's first words, his first steps, his first birthday, and many more after that.

He smiled as to how merciful the gods have been to him. Knowing there was an heir to succeed him was gratifying.

"Ebuka! Ebuka!" King Obeze yelled.

Ebuka came flying down the hall with his sword in its sheath around his waist.

"Ebuka, summon my son, Sọchima. I request his presence at once!"

"Yes, my king," Ebuka replied immediately and left to find Sọchima.

Sọchima approached the king's chambers and tapped on the door with his knuckles. He breathed heavily as he awaited a response from his father.

"The door is unlocked," King Obeze grunted from inside his chambers.

"Father, you sent for me!" Sọchima responded as he made his way inside the king's chambers.

 Sọchima was warmly embraced by his father.

King Obeze held onto Sọchima, placed a kiss on his forehead, and guided him to a chair.

"My son, I have watched you grow into a fine young man. I believe it is time I let you in on your duties as the future king of our great kingdom.

"You must be prepared, trained, and groomed on the manhood ceremonial rites. This ceremony is important and should have taken place when you turned sixteen"

"The manhood ritual has existed long before our forefathers, and every male child born into this kingdom must take part in it.

"Every young male of Ogbodo kingdom must pass through the rites before they are considered true men of the land. They must prove themselves man enough to earn the respect of a woman or to be called warriors and defenders of their land. Most importantly, they must be considered man enough to share a bed with a woman bride."

King Obeze concluded, "After your manhood initiation, we can begin to explore possible chances for your coronation as a crowned prince of this kingdom." King Obeze ended his speech with a chuckle.

Sọchima nodded with a grin of affirmation. "Well spoken, Father. Maazi Ukaonu did mention the manhood initiation rites to me but I was too busy with my bush meat traps and didn't pay much attention to him."

"Very well, son, I am glad that you are beginning to understand the ways of our people. Maazi Ukaonu was right to mention it to you. Let us plan for the next eke market day. I have spoken with the cabinet chiefs and with Maazi Ukaonu who is the custodian for the rites of manhood initiation. After your coronation as prince," King Obeze continued, "you will be free to choose a wife *from Ogbodo kingdom.*"

He threw a sharp glance at Sọchima who had a neutral expression on his face. He was a bit confused as he nodded his head in agreement with his father's words.

"Yes, Father, may all these be done according to the will of the gods."

"My son may the gods be praised! First and foremost, we must get you ready for the initiation rites into manhood."

CHAPTER FOURTEEN

The next eke market day had approached. Sọchima was being prepared for the initiation rites of manhood. It was always a thing of pride for the young youths who already had passed the initiation.

Ezemmuo was in an intense consultation with the gods. While the preparations were going on, Sọchima sneaked out to see Erimma, for she was the only maiden he could freely speak to without having to put on a bogus act.

Sọchima was scared and excited at the same time. He confronted his fears before Erimma and tried to assure her that he was going to be okay.

As they sneaked out through the back door, heading towards the courtyard, Erimma held Sọchima's hands and looked at him comfortingly.

"Chima, I am sure you are going to be okay! You are brave and strong," Erimma said with a smile as she gently squeezed Sọchima's hands. Sọchima smiled without saying a word. What he loved about her was her gentle nature and how softly she spoke.

"Thank you Mma for your kind words. I only wished the initiation took place when I was a baby, so I don't have to feel or remember what happens in it. My friends say it's not as comfortable as the elders make it sound." Sọchima gave a worried grimace.

"Perhaps not," Erimma affirmed. "Mbachi's brother went through the

117

rites and didn't say anything good about it either. I am sure you are going to be okay; I know that."

They both inspected the traps they had laid out the previous evening.

"You have your way with words, 'Mma, and you always know what to say to make me feel better. You make things right for me," Sọchima said as he squeezed her hand harder. Erimma avoided his eyes; she loved Sọchima, but only the gods could decide.

"Stop it, Sọchima, you flatter me a lot!" Erimma chuckled.

It was the evening of the same day, the day of the initiation rites ceremony.

The cabinet chiefs arrived at the palace, with Ezemmuo, to accompany Sọchima to the shrine. Maazi Ukaonu led the group of cabinet men, as the custodian of the manhood rites.

Sọchima was wrapped in a white cloth, and Maazi Ukaonu used white chalk to draw an image of a small pot on Sọchima's forehead.

The pot was meant to signify his destiny, which would be presented to the gods so they could fill the pot with blessings as he was about to become a man.

Sọchima carried a coconut with both hands. The water inside it would be given to him to drink during the initiation rites.

As they embarked on a path to the shrine, the procession was joined by Ogbodo boys. Their presence was to encourage Sọchima as he embarked on the journey. They cheered the paths with their songs and dancing.

Towards the end of the procession, King Obeze walked with his personal guard, Ebuka. Within the kingdom, young maidens prepared themselves as prospective brides, as Sọchima would be free to choose one after the initiation rites were over.

Some of the maidens already knew that Sọchima liked Erimma a lot; however, they also knew it was a futile relationship since Erimma, an Abaziani maiden, could not be married to a royal blood line in Ogbodo.

Queen Obiageli was excited as she was dressed in a beautiful patterned lace fabric with beads to match. She was excited that her little boy was becoming a man, and she awaited his return eagerly.

As the people approached the shrine of Ogbodo kingdom, Ezemmuo took the coconut from Sọchima and placed it inside a basket. He placed a white piece of feather at the back of Sọchima's ears and summoned him to kneel before the great god of fertility.

Ezemmuo chanted and danced around Sọchima, who was kneeling with both hands together in a downward position.

Maazi Ukaonu dabbed Sọchima's chest with a white cloth as Ezemmuo broke the coconut. He poured half of the coconut water on Sọchima's chest and gave him the other half to drink.

The coconut water would help to trigger an ejaculation sooner rather than later. While Sọchima brought himself to ejaculate, Ezemmuo chanted incantations to evoke the gods of fertility. Sọchima immersed his penis as fast as he could.

Within moments an ejaculation occurred. His sperm was taken by Ezemmuo and presented to the god of fertility, who in return blessed the participant with the providence of male and female children during procreation.

At the completion of the procedure, Sọchima was escorted back to the palace. King Obeze let out a sigh of relief as the event ended. He had prayed silently for the procedure to be over. King Obeze approached Sọchima and kissed his forehead.

"You are now a man, and the true son of your father!" King Obeze hailed Sọchima as he held him in an embrace.

As they arrived at the palace, Queen Obiageli rushed out to welcome her son. She cried in excitement as she pressed Sọchima against her breast in an embrace. "Welcome home, my son."

Sọchima smiled at his mother as he put his arms around her shoulders.

The maiden dance at the palace began with maidens hoping to be chosen as his bride. All Ogbodo maidens who wished to be married usually took part in the dance after the initiation into manhood rites.

After the day had come to a glorious end, Sọchima could not wait to retire to his chambers; he was exhausted from all the day's activity.

At the same time, he was happy with his remarkable progress and was eager to share all in detail with Erimma.

His coronation would be coming up shortly and that would be a good time to tell his parents he wanted Erimma as his bride. Maybe their union will bring the two communities together and abolish a tradition that forbade a royal line from marrying outside the kingdom. Sọchima wished!

Sọchima crawled into bed and dozed off.

CHAPTER FIFTEEN

Twenty market days had passed after the manhood initiation ceremony. It was the morning of Sọchima's coronation as the crown prince of Ogbodo kingdom.

Sọchima did not feel as though there was something huge about to happen to him again. He was so exhausted from the activities he had to do to learn the ways of kingship. All these happenings were keeping him away from his bush meat hunt.

The events and rituals of the manhood ceremony still played on his mind. Whilst Sọchima's mind was burdened with those thoughts, he could not get the flashing image of Erimma out of his head.

Sọchima's feelings towards Erimma were pure. But for his people: a taboo. Sọchima knew this was going to instigate a fight between him and the throne, that is, the king.

He was willing to fight for what he truly wanted, but only the gods would decide his fate. The traditions of the kingdom were burdensome. Sometimes Sọchima wished he were not born into a royal blood line.

His life would have been easier, and he'd have been free to live on his own terms. A life of hunting, farming, and loving Erimma was all he desired.

Prince Sọchima was hoping he could change certain traditions when he became king. People should be free to marry someone from any kingdom regardless of tribe, royal blood line or traditions, Sọchima thought.

The palace was being prepared for Sọchima's coronation. The fat cows had already been slaughtered, and about a hundred tubers of yam were already being cooked.

King Obeze and his queen were both getting ready for the coronation. The cabinet chiefs marched in pairs into the courtyard as they conversed, and they looked forward to the palm wine that they would drink.

Ebuka, the palace guard, was busy stacking up kegs of fresh palm wine; he had already stacked up one hundred gallons.

Meanwhile, while Sọchima was getting ready for the day's event, lost in his thoughts, he did not notice that the woven mat curtain to his inner chamber was open. Erimma quietly made her way into Sọchima's room.

She stood at the door not sure to proceed further or not. She gazed down the hall to ensure no one was watching.

Erimma cleared her throat, trying to get Sọchima's attention, for he was by now facing the window while he tied on his fabric.

"My love, I didn't hear you come in! How long have you been standing there?" Sọchima rushed to the door, pulled Erimma inside, and closed the door.

"Not too long, my love." Erimma smiled.

"Does anyone know you are here?" Sọchima asked, as he did not want Erimma getting into trouble for being inside his inner chambers.

"No one knows I am here; I just came to check up on you and wish you luck on your big day," Erimma said, beaming.

Sọchima pulled Erimma into his arms and caressed her back as he pressed his face to hers. Erimma broke out of his hold, for she could not look Sọchima in the face. She was beginning to cry as she made her way to the door.

"Wait! Wait! Do not go my love, I am sorry, I did not mean to do that!" Sọchima said as he grabbed Erimma's waist. She pressed her face into his chest and allowed the tears to flow down freely.

"I love you, Sọchima, but we cannot be together!" Erimma whispered as she sobbed.

"I want to make you my wife, my love. I know it's going to be a fight, but I plan to tell my parents about us after my coronation," Sọchima said, trying to sound encouraging.

Erimma did not say a word as she buried her face in Sọchima's arms and allowed him to caress her back. Sọchima grabbed her chin and gently sunk his tongue inside Erimma's mouth.

They kissed and moaned as the heat of passion possessed their hungry bodies. Sọchima gently guided Erimma back onto the wooden bed. Each touch was magical, and they both cried as Sọchima thrust himself inside of her, making Erimma moan between sobs.

"We can be together, my love!" Sọchima whispered as he penetrated between Erimma's thighs.

He grabbed her intensely as he guided his hands onto her breasts.

"Tonight, I become the crowned prince, and soon Erimma, daughter of Maazi Obigwe of Abaziani, will be my bride and my queen."

They both laughed and held onto each other tightly.

Now, on the evening of the coronation, Ezemmuo had already finished the cleansing rites in the palace.

King Obeze summoned Sọchima to give the youth his blessings and then handed him over to Ezemmuo and the cabinet chiefs. They took Sọchima through the royal rites and the oath to uphold the leadership of the kingdom.

After the necessary procedures had taken place, Ezemmuo began to decorate Sọchima with neck and ankle beads while muttering incantations.

"Great people of Ogbodo! Behold your prince! The one that is to take over after the reign of his father!

Prince Sọchima Ubaka of Ogbodo kingdom!" Ezemmuo cried out to the people. They cheered in jubilation and excitement. This was followed with masquerade performances and the maiden dance which brought the day to a close.

CHAPTER SIXTEEN

Fourteen market days had passed since the coronation of Prince Sọchima. Being a crowned prince meant he had to give up his bush meat traps in exchange for countless meetings with the cabinet chiefs.

Prince Sọchima would have preferred his bush meat trap escapades to the countless meetings he had to sit through and observe the proceedings of in preparation for kingship, for when his father, King Obeze, joined his ancestors.

Prince Sọchima's mind drifted as he sat amongst the elders in a meeting with the cabinet chiefs; the thought of

Erimma triggered a rush of excitement in the young prince.

He smiled as he allowed his thoughts to wander around the deep intensifying erotic moments that he had shared with her.

He could not get that image out of his mind. He realised he has not seen Erimma since after the coronation.

She was almost always at the front yard of the Queen's chambers attending to Queen's Obiageli's needs. Prince Sọchima wondered if everything was well with Erimma. She would not usually stay away in that manner unless something was wrong.

Queen Obiageli, though now showing signs of aging, was still beautiful and well adorned in the glory of a queen. As she carefully tended to her plants, she made sure they were without weeds. The queen cared for them the way a mother would care for her child.

Everyone in the palace knew that she overfed the plants with so much water and manure. Her love for the plants knew no bounds. She would spend hours trimming and cutting until she was satisfied with the outlook.

Prince Sọchima left the meeting arena with the elders and made his way to the queen's chambers. He had not seen a lot of his mother lately either. If anyone should know the whereabouts of Erimma, it would be his mother, as Erimma was the queen's personal maid and steward.

"Mother may your days be long," Sọchima greeted the queen as he planted a kiss on her forehead.

"My son, it's so good to see you."

"I haven't seen much of you since after your coronation," Queen Obiageli said as she searched through Sọchima's thoughts with her eyes. She knew the young man was troubled.

"Mother, it's been one meeting after another since the coronation. I no longer have time to attend to my traps! I was hoping Erimma could help me with those. Have you seen her lately?" Sọchima tried to avoid his mother's eyes.

Queen Obiageli smiled while trying to maintain a firm look on her face.

"My son, I have watched you two grow up together in this palace, and I know how fond of each other you both are. Remember you are a crowned prince now, and you should concern yourself with kingship duties, not bush meat traps."

"Mother, I am not just fond of her, I love her!" Sọchima snapped.

He let out a deep breath as he held Queen Obiageli's hands.

He knew he might have upset her. Sọchima knew the only way to win Erimma's hand in marriage was by trying to get his mother on his side.

The queen spoke softly and tearfully. "My son may your father never hear of this! I knew it would come to this!

I hope you know that Erimma is a maiden from Abaziani and that you are from a royal blood line. You know our traditions will not allow you marry a maiden from Abaziani!"

Prince Sọchima nodded calmly but with a feeling of disappointment.

"Mother, please talk to Father on my behalf! He needs to know how I feel," Prince Sọchima pleaded with Queen Obiageli, as he knelt before her and pressed his face against her palms.

"My son, it is not in my place to make such an abominable plea; it's against everything that we believe in," Queen Obiageli said in a rather sorrowful tone.

"Okay! Mother, where is Erimma? I have not seen her in a while," Prince

Sọchima asked as he focused his gaze on his mother.

Queen Obiageli stood still for a while; she was not comfortable with answering questions concerning Erimma since it had become more of a controversial discussion.

At last she admitted, "My son, Erimma was sent home to Abaziani! The palace maidens reported her of being ill." Queen Obiageli began to pull weeds.

"She has refused meals until she became weak and pale. Some say she may be with child. Abaziani has the best herbal options to help with her ailment. We await news from Abaziani, and she will return when she feels better."

Prince Sọchima was speechless, unable to find words, he felt so angry, confused, and disappointed.

"And no one thought it right to tell me this!" Prince Sọchima raged in an angry tone. "Mother, if Erimma is with child, that child is mine!"

Queen Obiageli felt like she had just been given a hurtful slap. She was astonished and terrified. Everything had just gone wrong.

"I shall speak to my father at once!" Prince Sọchima stormed out of the room, leaving his mother dazed.

While King Obeze was in the confines of a meeting with the cabinet chiefs, Prince Ṣọchima made a remarkable entrance. There was an unexpected silence in the room. The cabinet chiefs glared at each other while waiting for the king to speak first.

"My son, you have just interrupted a meeting in progress. What is it that troubles you with indignation?" King Obeze asked with an embarrassed look on his face.

"Father, my elders! I am sorry for disrupting the meeting. I just need to know about the maiden servant, Erimma, from Abaziani," Prince Ṣọchima said politely.

"You mean the maiden that was sent home? News came back from Abaziani that she was pregnant with

144

child," King Obeze replied
shockingly.

"Yes Father! I love her, Father! The
child she carries is my child!" Prince
Sọchima exclaimed as he fell at the
king's feet and held onto the king
pleadingly.

King Obeze released himself from
Sọchima's hold. The cabinet chiefs
all cried out in loud voices. There was
confusion and chattering in the room.

"Sọchima! What have you done?"
King Obeze asked in bewilderment
and anger.

"May the gods of our land heal our
ears from what we just heard," Maazi
Ukaonu bellowed, and he folded
both arms underneath his armpits.

"A royal seed cannot be living outside
the confines of a royal wall! A royal

seed conceived by a woman from Abaziani! TUFIAKWA! What an abominable act!" Maazi Ibeka retorted in a loud voice.

"What calamity! What impertinence! Summon Ezemmuo," King Obeze commanded.

Queen Obiageli, who by now had shown up in the throne room, was already sobbing with grief. It was not her place to decide the fate of the maiden and the unborn child. She quietly returned to her chambers and wished there were something she could do to save the situation.

"Sọchima!" King Obeze yelled. "Sọchima, son of King Obeze and Queen Obiageli of Ogbodo kingdom, I decree that Erimma is banished from this land and never to set foot in it until death. Her actions have

146

brought calamity upon our land and on our people!" King Obeze's face contorted with disgust. His eyes filled with anger like those of an angry lion.

"No, Father, you cannot do this!" Prince Sọchima screamed and cried as he begged King Obeze, who by now had dismissed the cabinet chiefs and demanded to be called upon when Ezemmuo arrived.

CHAPTER SEVENTEEN

Ogbodo kingdom was in obvious disarray over the events of the previous days. Everyone talked in hushed whispers about the banishment of Erimma. The people of Abaziani serving in the kingdom of Ogbodo all packed up and left in fury.

How could Erimma be banished just like that? She served the kingdom of Ogbodo all throughout her childhood; it was the place that she called home. Was it right that she had to pay the price for a grievous offence that was committed by two consenting adults?

All these questions had no right or wrong answers, but the people of

Abaziani and Ogbodo kingdom pondered within themselves the courage to speak up for what was right.

Prince So̩chima had known no peace since the banishment of Erimma and his unborn child. He hardly touched his food nor checked his bush meat traps as he fondly had done with Erimma, and he spoke to no one, especially not his farther, the king.

Queen Obiageli was distraught with the recent happenings in the palace. In her confused state, she wished there were something she could do to avert the wrath of the gods that was coming down upon the entire kingdom. She knew this day would come, the day the gods finally decided to speak and act.

The visit of Ezemmuo to the palace had made matters worse, leaving more questions than answers. The messenger of the gods spoke of impending doom and disaster since it was an abomination for a royal child to be growing outside the confines of the palace and the royal bloodline.

However, Erimma was nowhere to be found after the news of the banishment reached Abaziani. While the people of Abaziani controlled most of the farming and food trade in the kingdom of Ogbodo, their sudden exit meant that there was a shortage of food within the kingdom of Ogbodo.

The farming season was around the corner, and contingency plans were put in place as the kingdom tried to overcome the calamity that was about to befall them.

Ezemmuo shook his head in uncontrollable disappointment as he glanced to the skies in search of answers from the gods. He moved his shoulders vigorously as he blew out the light in his old rusted lantern.

"May the gods forbid; I shall make it to the place by first light," Ezemmuo snapped.

The banishment of Erimma was a concern for Ezemmuo, as he already knew that the king was quick to anger in his decision to get rid of the maiden and the unborn child.

Prince Sọchima's anxiety grew like that of a woman in the pangs of labour. He became more and more restless each day as he wondered about Erimma. Are they still alive? The feelings overwhelmed Sọchima's mind.

He quickly grabbed his neatly handcrafted shoulder bag and put in a few wrappers, a drinking jar, his sword, and his pistol. He made his way to the queen's chambers, letting himself in without knocking. Queen Obiageli sat in the foyer watching her plants.

"Greetings, Mother," Sọchima said as he strolled into her arms for a warm embrace.

"My son may the gods keep you. Are you going hunting today?" Queen Obiageli asked, smiling to see her son becoming himself again.

"No Mother, I am going out in search of my child and Erimma. Tell no one, including Father, but if I am not back in three market days, you can tell him I am gone. I cannot live like this anymore! I need to do something!" Sọchima cried.

Queen Obiageli dropped her water vase and reached out to Sọchima as she pressed her body against his.

"My son, it is too dangerous out there. At least take a guard," Queen Obiageli stammered.

She searched for the right words to make Prince Sọchima change his mind, but she knew there was nothing she could do to stop him.

"Your father will be very angry," Queen Obiageli yelled.

"I don't care! My father cares for no one except for himself," Prince

Sọchima fumed as he made his way through the door.

"My son, he is still your farther and the king," Queen Obiageli cautioned him. "If you must go, may the gods watch over you," Queen Obiageli said in a calm but anxious manner.

"Thank you, Mother." Prince Sọchima kissed his mother on the forehead and quickly dashed out of the room.

CHAPTER EIGHTEEN

King Obeze spent most of his time within the confines of his royal chambers immersed in the darkness of his thoughts and emotions and pondering recent happenings inside and outside of the kingdom.

He was at war with himself, and knew no peace, becoming angry at every slightest provocation. Aside from when he performed his royal duties, he barely left his chambers.

Queen Obiageli avoided him like the plague as he blamed her for Sọchima's sudden departure.

"I couldn't stop him, my king; his mind was already made up when he came to me," Queen Obiageli would always say each time King Obeze blamed her for letting the prince go.

The people of Abaziani had not been on good terms ever since the banishment of Erimma. All food and livestock had been fully withdrawn from Ogbodo kingdom.

The king wondered if the only thing left to do was declare war. The last thing Ogbodo kingdom needed to worry about was going into war with Abaziani.

There would not be any survivors if that should ever happen, because both the men and women of Abaziani were warriors.

The people of Abaziani sent delegates to renegotiate the terms of justice on behalf of their daughter, Erimma.

King Obeze grudgingly came out of his inner chambers to preside over the meeting.

The meeting was supposed to be reasonably peaceful and agreeable, but it turned into roaring madness as no one was willing to listen to the opposing side. There was no mutual agreement on the decisions taken. Engulfed in anger, King Obeze stormed out of the meeting and declared it finished.

While things were heating up between the two kingdoms, Prince Sọchima wandered the forest of Amaniko endlessly, in search of Erimma and his unborn child.

People that suffered banishment mostly ended up in the forest of Amaniko; some made it to the neighboring kingdom of Ijakwu; the unlucky ones passed out in the forest and were eaten by wild beasts.

After three days, the prince still had not found any sign of Erimma nor her dead body. Maybe she made it to the next village of Ijakwu, or maybe she could be in the tribe of Iloka, Sọchima thought.

The village of Iloka was several miles away and it would take a day and a half to get there if the prince did not run out of food and water.

Spending another night in the forest was not a good idea, as Prince Sọchima's body had already become food for mosquitos and insects. Prince Sọchima decided to walk further up into the forest towards the direction leading to the village of Iloka, hoping to get as far as possible before night fall.

The village Iloka was the only village within reachable distance from the forest of Amaniko. Prince Sọchima was sure Erimma would have gone that way. With mixed feelings of hope and uncertainty, the prince feared arriving in the village only to discover Erimma was not there.

As he moved deeper and deeper into the forest, he saw foot tracks; many people had come by that route, but he was not sure if the tracks led to anywhere. As he walked by each track, he dropped a cowry into it to determine the pattern of the tracks and to retrace his steps if he needed to head back.

Every step he took along the tracks brought him a glimmer of hope, although he might be walking into a trap or a bait or even to Erimma. Whatever it was, Prince Sọchima needed to find out.

Whatever was ahead, he was walking that path of his free choice; it was his destiny and something he would live to tell of or else die.

Time had passed since the prince of Ogbodo kingdom fled in search of Erimma and the unborn child. Queen Obiageli tended to her plants in great emotional distress, as the thought of Sọchima kept her awake all day and night.

She reflected on the happenings in the kingdom within the past weeks; the fear of losing everything made her terrified. She feared that moment of truth which would not have arisen if Sọchima had not fallen into a forbidden relationship.

Queen Obiageli loved her family and was willing to do anything to protect the dignity and principles that the Ubaka dynasty had held over time.

No solution to the impending doom came to her mind. She thought that Sọchima was probably lost, wandering the forests without guards or maidens.

King Obeze was not making things better for Queen Obiageli, as he blamed her for all that had happened. Queen Obiageli avoided the king desperately since she did not want to get into a fight with him over Sọchima's disappearance.

Queen Obiageli spent most of her time in the company of her friend, Ifeoma. They would tend to the plants together, while Ifeoma would try to get the queen's mind off of Sọchima with her endless jokes.

Queen Obiageli would laugh at Ifeoma's jokes, yet she would still appear to be absent-minded, rapidly drifting into her thoughts.

"I feel like you have not been listening to me, my queen," Ifeoma broke into the queen's thoughts.

Ifeoma and Queen Obiageli had been best friends since their maiden days, and Ifeoma knew the queen even better than king Obeze did.

During their maiden days, King Obeze would give Ifeoma cracked palm kernel to take to Obiageli as he was too shy to meet with her. Ifeoma did not mind being the middleman between her best friend and King Obeze. She was an outspoken woman and an extrovert.

While Ifeoma was playing middleman for Queen Obiageli and King Obeze, she met and fell in love with Obika, the chief guard of King Chigbo Ubaka, who was the late king and father of King Obeze.

Obika was a strong handsome man who retired after King Chigbo died. Obika's son Ebuka began serving King Obeze as the chief guard.

Queen Obiageli and Ifeoma finally finished with the plants. They washed their hands vigorously and walked back into the queen's royal chambers.

Ifeoma wished there were something more she could do to make her friend feel better. Queen Obiageli was happy to have Ifeoma by her side, although she was too troubled and distraught about her son to tell Ifeoma this.

CHAPTER NINETEEN

Only one good thing came out of the meeting between the delegates from Abaziani and the king's counselors in Ogbodo. Both parties agreed not to pursue war against each other by virtue of the community ties that they had always shared. If that were not the case, Ogbodo kingdom would not stand any chance of survival. The warriors of Abaziani fought like wild beasts.

As King Obeze sipped from his cup of fresh palm wine, each gulp reminded him of the pain the past few weeks have brought upon him. No matter how much hope he had tried to embrace, his anguish was made greater. He suffered from the pain of not knowing if he still had a son or not, and the pain of an impending outcome looming in the dark.

King Obeze had already sent Ebuka to get Ezemmuo as soon as the first light broke out. His restlessness and lack of sleep was becoming a concern.

A toad would not run around during the day unless it was being chased by something. When it did, it was a sign of an imminent disaster. That was the kind of feeling King Obeze had.

Obeze needed Ezemmuo to bring him good news from the gods on the whereabouts of his son, good news about restoring peace to the lands, and information about which sacrifices were needed to do all that.

Ebuka, the palace guard, arrived with Ezemmuo just in time as King Obeze was about to take the last gulp of his palm wine.

King Obeze cleared his throat as he gently placed the cup down and gestured to Ebuka to leave the room.

Ezemmuo moved from one corner of the throne room to another, observing the markings on the wall and vocalizing words of incantation.

The king said, "Ezemmuo, the eyes of the gods, the messenger from above and beyond. What a man standing up cannot see, you, Ezemmuo, can see sitting down! My troubled heart takes sleep away from my eyes. What can I do to restore peace to my soul and to my kingdom?"

Ezemmuo shook his head abruptly, stared at king Obeze for a while with a sigh, then settled down on the floor, tucking his legs under his thighs.

Ezemmuo stretched out both hands, resting them on his kneecaps. With a terrifying look on his face, Ezemmuo spoke calmly. "The gods are angry! Darkness supersedes light. The mouth is weak to speak, and the tongue too heavy to carry the words. The shoulders are too feeble to carry the burden and weight of karma that lies ahead.

"The disappearance of an heir is evident, but the banishment of your bloodline is a curse and is sacrilegious to the throne; of this, I shall speak no more.

"Gather the cabinet chiefs, on the next eke market day, and I shall return."

Ezemmuo ended his words with a distinctive head nod, assembled his incantation tools, and left the palace.

King Obeze listened in terror, feeling as though his heart was being ripped out of his chest; his jaws hung slack, but no words came out.

The king's mind rampaged through the words of Ezemmuo in total confusion. He thought, why does Ezemmuo need the cabinet chiefs to be summoned? What does Ezemmuo know about my past? All these questions triggered fear and uncertainty in King Obeze's psyche. The day felt longer than normal with all these revelations sweeping through his mind.

"The gods must be angry!" King Obeze exclaimed as he paced his rooms. Banishment of one's bloodline? My bloodline? A message with great consequence!

Moreover, he had never banished Sọchima, and he knew Sọchima was not of his blood either, so what implication could that hold in Ezemmuo's words?

The more King Obeze thought of these words, the more confused he became.

"Ebuka!" King Obeze raged out. "Summon my wife, the queen."

As Queen Obiageli approached the king's chambers, she knew that something was wrong. Everything had been bad since the day King Obeze banished the young maiden, and the day that Sọchima vanished in search of her.

"My Lord," Queen Obiageli said, attempting to break the silence in the room.

"My queen, I think the gods are onto us!" King Obeze said as he sat up from his chair in an agitated state.

"My king, you speak in parables; your words are heavy, yet vicious," Queen Obiageli responded in a trembling manner as she sat beside the king.

"Ezemmuo was here; he spoke in fables, yet his words felt real but confusing. The message seemed clear yet unclear, and he spoke about a banished bloodline, something that makes absolutely no sense to me. Ezemmuo will return on the next eke market day with the chiefs in council."

Queen Obiageli cried profusely, beating her breast so hard that her skin turned pale. "My king, Sọchima has awoken the gods upon us! Our past is finally here to take its revenge!"

Queen Obiageli heaved a sigh of desperation.

"Enough! Enough! Stop!" King Obeze barked. "I summoned you here for solutions, and not lamentations! What should we do? Crying will not solve the impending disaster!"

Queen Obiageli tried to calm herself down. She sat slumped with worry, clenching both fists. "I think we should summon Nnejekwu the midwife from Abaziani to give us more insight on the birth of Sọchima," Queen Obiageli said as she looked away into thin air.

"That sounds like a good place to start, but we already know all we need to know about Sọchima. How will bringing up old stories help our situation right now?"

The queen did not say a word, but sat still, dwelling in her thoughts.

The king concluded abruptly, "I will summon Ebuka to go down to Abaziani and fetch Nnejekwu! Hopefully, she still lives, but we have not seen or heard from her for almost nineteen years."

"We may find some answers that we seek," Queen Obiageli said reassuringly.

CHAPTER TWENTY

It had been six months since Prince Sọchima left Ogbodo kingdom. He could hardly recognise himself. Life outside of the palace had been difficult and uncertain. Moving from one community to the next in search of Erimma was beginning to seem impossible. Sọchima's attempt to find Erimma was to no avail.

She is probably dead, he thought as he walked through Awoja forest.

It was his sixteenth stop so far in search of Erimma. Prince Sọchima was, by now, very far away from home; most of the kingdoms he stopped by hardly knew nor recognised him as a prince, or even knew about his kingdom.

Prince Sọchima stopped by the stream of Awoja for a drink. His skills in hunting had kept him alive, for he relied on hunting livestock and animals for food. Prince Sọchima's traps were highly efficient and caught the forest's finest animals.

He made traps in the way he had learned from Ugboko, the great hunter of Ogbodo kingdom.

Prince Sọchima grew to be more independent and relied heavily on his skills and human instincts. While Sọchima persisted in searching for Erimma and the child, he also thought about his aging mother, Queen Obiageli, and the pain she must be experiencing because of his absence. Prince Sọchima loved his mother but finding Erimma was his priority.

With much hesitation and doubt, Prince Sọchima reached a building that looked like an old ancestral home within the clan of Awoja and the boundary of Iweha kingdom.

The clan of Awoja was popularly known to have great seers and psychics. The great Ujankita of Awoja was known to be a deity that predicted the future. He would see things before they happened. During the days of the forefathers, it was known that people would go to Ujankita to know their destiny and curses. This offered the people the privilege of trying to avert curses with endless sacrifices and ancestral prayers. Women visited the shrine to know the destiny of their unborn children.

Prince Sọchima knew he had reached the right place to find out the whereabouts of Erimma and his child. He was unsure of how he ended up in Awoja, as he had walked the forests and kingdoms aimlessly for the past six months.

Finding himself in the shrine of Ujankita was the will of the gods. Prince Sọchima smiled as a glimmer of hope lit his thoughts. As he approached the crumbling old mud hut, he feared for his life, as he was unsure who was lurking in the corners. Thus, he stepped behind a shrub to hide.

Not everyone who came as far as Ujankita's shrine has made it out in one piece.

Although the place seemed dead upon arrival, without any sign of human life, Prince Sọchima knew someone was within the confines of the hut, or at least around the shrine.

Prince Sọchima raised his feet up after each step in order not to give away his hiding spot. He peeped through the leaves by raising his head up a little bit in between the shrub's leaves.

"Take one step further, and your legs shall leave your body."

The voice of Ichokiri, the chief priest of Ujankita shrine of Awoja kingdom, cried out.

Prince Sọchima quickly lowered his head back inside the shrubs. He crawled quietly, with his bare hands crunching the leaves, to the other side of the mango tree. Although he was scared, he knew he must defend himself no matter what was threatening him.

Prince Sọchima confronted his fears and stood up from his hiding spot.

"Wise one, I come in peace!" Prince Sọchima said with both hands up in the air in surrender. "I am a common wanderer in search of my loved one and child."

Prince Sọchima slowly advanced towards Ichokiri.

The chief priest stared at Sọchima as he put his knife down, and he beckoned Prince Sọchima to follow him. In silence, they approached the entrance door to the mud hut that had been patched with mats of woven leaves and stems.

Ichokiri guided Sọchima to an old wooden bench outside of the hut. As

Sọchima carefully settled onto the half-broken bench, he wondered if this was the end of the road to his trouble of finding Erimma.

Ichokiri performed some rituals; he was never known as a man with many words and was known not to speak to mortals unless he had a message or a revelation from the gods. He was believed to be a god himself; that is, half human and half god.

People believed that whoever made it as far as Awoja shrine never departed without answers and resolutions to their problems. Unfortunately, not many people made it out alive.

The forest of Awoja was thick and dangerous. The dead roamed around, as spirits and wild beasts procreated.

Ichokiri lifted his hands up in the air and danced around the great statue of Ujankita with a melodic chant of praise. Ichokiri was known to see one's problem even before they arrived or spoke about it.

Suddenly he said, "Indeed, the gods have awakened. Indeed, my dreams and visions are clearer now to behold the mystery of a lost royal bloodline! The cry of an innocent child, the tears of a lost maiden; yet, the persistence of a man in love knows no bounds."

Ichokiri continued to speak in both clear and mystical words. Prince Sọchima knelt and bowed his head before the great shrine as he patiently waited for the revelation of his destiny to be complete.

The prince felt trickles of sweat rolling down his armpits; he was both hopeful and nervous that this may be the beginning or the end to his journey.

"My son, your child and the maiden live! Both have returned to the great land of Abaziani. The maiden is still with child but in hiding for fear of the child's death if found. Be wise my son but make haste while the sun still shines."

With both hope and desperation renewed, Sọchima set out for Abaziani. It all felt like a dream. Those months wandering and the pain he went through all felt worth it now that he knew there might be a glimpse of light at the end of this dark tunnel.

He wondered why Erimma travelled back to Abaziani! She must have roamed the forests before making her way back home. It was not easy to survive out there alone and pregnant. Or maybe she travelled back home so that he could find her?

Maybe she heard or now knew that he went in search of her?

All these questions rampaged through the mind of the prince. It would take him at least five market days to reach Abaziani if he maintained a quick pace. As Prince Ṣọchima walked back, he wondered where in Abaziani Erimma could be hiding. The prince knew that once he reached Abaziani, it would be easier to narrow down the search from there. Erimma may likely have headed towards her paternal grandmother's village in Abaziani, as she always talked about her village with Prince Ṣọchima.

Ṣọchima also knew he needed to hide as well, to not be seen by the people until he found Erimma and ensured her safety. The prince knew his father could be quick to anger and could order the child taken or even killed if there were sightings of Erimma in Abaziani.

As nightfall approached, Ṣọchima found a place he could snooze. He used his knife to cut down a few palm leaves and carefully placed them on the ground underneath a guava tree. He lay there with his bag as a pillow to support his head, and he dozed off.

With the fine tone of the morning birds, Prince Sọchima woke up feeling as if he had never slept. The night was very short. He was tired, but knew the journey ahead was still long.

As he forced himself to get up, he imagined what his itinerary for the day would be like. Weather permitting, he could cross the river before the tide rose. Heading east, the prince approached the boundaries between Ugbo and Ebute kingdoms. Ugbo kingdom was known for a good hunt.

Prince Sọchima endured the hunger that was already ripping him apart. His reward could probably be nice fat, roasted, bush meat from Ugbo forest, although the weather did not look promising for a good catch. Despite the intense hunger taunting

Prince Sọchima, all he could think of
was seeing Erimma again.

If only Erimma knew how much he
has yearned for her love! Thinking of
holding her in his arms again, Prince
Sọchima's face lit up in a warm smile.

Hopefully Erimma would not think
that he had abandoned her. By now
she must have heard of Prince
Sọchima missing from the kingdom
of Ogbodo. Maybe she would guess
that Prince Sọchima was lost inside
the forests in search of her.

As Prince Sọchima finally
approached Ebute community, he
settled down under a palm tree to
build and set up his traps. Once that
was done, he gathered leaves, wood,
and shrubs to make a fire for his
roast. It would probably take half an
hour for his trap to catch the

unfortunate bush meat that would serve as his lunch and dinner.

After catching and roasting his food, the prince felt stronger again. He crossed the river and increased his pace enough to cover some distance before nightfall. Prince Sọchima knew he was getting closer to his destination with each step.

He finally began to approach the border between Abaziani and Ngede, which was about three rivers away. While it had taken him months to find an answer to his pursuit, it would take him days to get back to the woman he loved. He was happy as each step he took brought him closer to home; for him, home was in the arms of Erimma.

CHAPTER TWENTY-ONE

King Obeze sent Ebuka to fetch Nnejekwu to the palace. He had to wait seven market days for her arrival, as her

health was failing. To make the trip, she had to be accompanied by her daughter, Ijemma, and her granddaughter, Ifechi.

Her presence at the palace was arduous for King Obeze and Queen Obiageli, as it aroused memories of past and buried deeds surrounding Sọchima, who was still nowhere to be found around the kingdom. However, her presence was vital in unraveling certain mysteries that surrounded Ezemmuo's prophetic revelations from the gods.

As Nnejekwu sat in the royal chambers, she looked around the room that had many memories. Nothing much had changed within the walls of the royal chamber. Nnejekwu pressed her elbow on her walking stick as she waited patiently for King Obeze to emerge from his private chambers.

King Obeze made an appearance accompanied by Queen Obiageli!

"Greetings to the king and queen of Ogbodo kingdom," the women greeted, as Ifechi and Ijemma knelt before the king.

"Greetings, daughters of Abaziani! Welcome to my kingdom," King Obeze responded with a hand pat on their backs. He beckoned towards the women to arise and sit down.

"Greetings to the king and queen of Ogbodo kingdom," Nnejekwu spoke in a weak and frail voice.

"You are welcome, mother of all children. I heard of your failing health, and I pray to the gods for better health for you," Queen Obiageli said to Nnejekwu with a tone of empathy.

The king commanded, "Ebuka, take the ladies to the courtyard; I need to speak to Nnejekwu alone."

"My king, it is no longer news that the prince has left the palace. I was sorry to hear that. May the gods bring him back safely," Nnejekwu said.

King Obeze nodded in silence. The thought of Prince Sọchima gone, with no news of life or death, sent an exhausted rush of fatigue through the king's mind.

King Obeze cleared his throat. "As to the disappearance of my son, my kingdom has known no peace, and my reign is being threatened by uncertainties.

"I was hoping that you could help me understand and throw more light on the birth of my son, Sọchima! Ezemmuo keeps stating there is a banishment of a royal bloodline." King Obeze was unsure if he had said all he needed to.

Nnejekwu began to sob quietly, struggling to find words as the tears burned her eyes. "My king, for so many years, I have prayed for this day to come. I thank the gods that death didn't come first." Nnejekwu's voice trembled.

"Nnejekwu, you speak in parables. If there is anything you have to say, say it! My patience is burning out." King Obeze used a steady tone, as he was working extremely hard to control his anger.

Nnejekwu continued, "Indeed, the gods have awakened. Indeed, here lies the answers to a thousand questions. This is the day I see before I die, the day my mouth speaks the truth, the truth too heavy to be spoken, only for the bravest of heart." Nnejekwu ranted as she beat her chest vigorously.

"Speak, woman! Speak!" King Obeze yelled.

She said, "Many years ago, after the birth of Sọchima, a woman named Nneoma, an Umuokpo maiden, came back to the orphanage in search of her child. She desired to know where her child lived.

"Nneoma narrated how she had fled her father's house on the day that was supposed to be her wedding as she was being forced to marry a man she did not want. She fled into the forest of Umuokpo.

"There she met a man whom she described as an unknown stranger, from Ogbodo kingdom, and it was shortly after the death of the previous king of Ogbodo kingdom."

Nnejekwu paused to look at the queen, then continued talking in her frail unsteady voice.

"While they were in the forest, she got laid by the man. Shortly after that, she realised she was pregnant. Her family abandoned her and the child, and cursed them, wanting never to set their eyes on her again for bringing shame and dishonor to the family.

"At that point, she came to the orphanage where she gave birth to the baby, and she fled shortly after. That baby is the boy prince that lives with you."

King Obeze was stunned! He stood up from his chair and paced the room in terror!

"Nnejekwu! You said this woman's name is Nneoma? A maiden from Umuokpo?"

"Yes, my king, her name is Nneoma," Nnejekwu replied with a glare of confusion.

"My king, is everything alright?" Queen Obiageli asked as she sat up in her chair, trying hard not to panic.

"Nnejekwu, what you just told me is different from what you told me many years ago when I asked you about the mother of the child!" King Obeze said in his confusion.

Nnejekwu explained, "My king, I am sorry, but now we know the truth. I only recounted to you the version that Nneoma told me many years ago. She came back with a new version of the story which I have just told you, and which she swore with her life was the truth."

"I am finished! It's over!" King Obeze cried out. "Indeed, the gods have awoken! Sọchima has awoken the gods! My queen, I am sorry! Forgive me!"

Fear filled King Obeze's eyes. Queen Obiageli began to sob quietly, unsure what news lay behind the king's words.

King Obeze narrated how he met Nneoma inside the forest of Umuokpo right near the border between Abaziani and Umuokpo. He told how he fled Ogbodo after the death of his father, King Chigbo Ubaka. King Obeze confessed how in his vulnerable state he had carnal knowledge of Nneoma.

"Never did I know that my seed was planted inside of her. Never did I know that she bore my son who came back to me as an adopted son," King Obeze said as he buried his face in his hands.

Now King Obeze understood the mystery of the banished bloodline from Ezemmuo's prophesy. "An abominable act! An act he orchestrated!"

How was he to face his people, the cabinet chiefs, his wife, and Sọchima, his biological son, as well?

By banishing Erimma, he had banished his grandchild, a royal bloodline. King Obeze banished Erimma because of her conceiving a child with Prince Sọchima, whereas he got an Umuokpo maiden pregnant and bore a child by her.

How had he been unable to admit this to his own sin before casting out another for the same sin?

If only he had known all of this before! He had banished Erimma because he did not think that Sọchima had an actual blood tie with him.

Queen Obiageli stood up and walked out from the room. She was upset that the king had not told her about his encounter with Nneoma. It was already wrong to have any dealing with a maiden that was not from Ogbodo kingdom but having a child with a maiden from another kingdom was worse, and the final straw was that the king had not told her.

"Nnejekwu, where is Nneoma now?" King Obeze asked.

Nnejekwu, feeling uneasy, replied, "My king, Nneoma passed away seven market days ago."

CHAPTER TWENTY-TWO

With the news of Nneoma's demise, King Obeze was devastated.

There was much on his mind that he wanted to say to Nneoma now that the truth was clear about the child.

If only he'd known that she had carried his child; maybe things would have turned out differently. Maybe Sọchima would still be here, although Sọchima's action was due to Obeze's irrepressible anger towards Erimma.

Living with the guilt, lies, and deception towards his kingdom, King Obeze was on the verge of losing everything, including his queen who had refused to speak to him after the revelation from Nnejekwu.

While the kingdom was still in great despair over the disappearance of the heir apparent, if the news of the gruesome discovery spread, there would be chaos.

The truth could no longer be hidden from the people. Now that the king knew the cause of the issue at hand, he needed to consult with Ezemmuo and the cabinet chiefs as to the way forward.

Queen Obiageli had remained silent over the disappearance of Sọchima as she pondered all of this in her heart. Her failing health had deteriorated since the day of the great revelation by Nnejekwu. Her heart was burdened by the fact that her husband could hide such a deed from her.

She would not have stopped him from marrying Nneoma.

Ezemmuo had been in and out of the palace on several occasions. The chief priest did not look very surprised when the news of the confession reached his ears.

"No matter how deep the ocean is, there is an end to its depth," he said. "When a mother hen abandons her chick and flees, then death is imminent for her chicks. Indeed, the gods have awoken! Only the truth shall prevail! Light and darkness do not mingle, but, amid darkness, light prevails. As the gods have decreed! The heir apparent lives."

Ezemmuo felt there was a glimmer of hope for the people of Ogbodo kingdom.

The knowledge of Sọchima being alive, coming from the messenger of the gods, was a huge relief in the kingdom. King Obeze was happy about that revelation, although he had a lot of work to do towards restoring peace in the land.

The cabinet chiefs have been working with the king to ensure that matters did not escalate.

Through some shimmer of hope, King Obeze wondered where Sọchima could be. If Sọchima was alive, why hadn't he come home yet? Could he be lost, or just wandering the forest of Omenuko? King Obeze pondered.

The forest of Omenuko was known to be one of the largest endless stretches of forestry joining the boarders of about seven kingdoms.

Only hunters who knew their way across the forest made it out alive. One could easily get lost in there and die.

Sọchima was good at hunting and farming, so if he ever ended up in the forest, he might be able to retrace his steps.

King Obeze's thoughts ran wild with the image of Sọchima as he prepared for his meeting. King Obeze was scheduled to address the people on all that had happened and how they all had ended up in the mess they were in now.

The king hoped that confessing and addressing the people would earn him forgiveness which, he hoped optimistically, would lead to Sọchima coming home. He was also anticipating the gesture would aid in restoring the queen's failing health through the mercy of the gods.

King Obeze knew that admitting his failings and shortcomings before his people was a difficult thing to do; those actions would present him as a humble king willing to do the bidding of the gods.

As much as King Obeze knew that desperation of an heir had instigated all that had happened, he wished he had done things differently, in an honourable way. Now he had the daunting option of standing before the people and saying things he never imagined he would say.

The message from the gods was very clear.

King Obeze had a choice to speak up and bear the consequences of his actions, or to remain silent and face the wrath of the gods. Obeze knew the only way to restore peace to the kingdom was to acknowledge his inadequacies, and to seek forgiveness.

He knew that he needed to give up his dignity to do that.

King Obeze silently prayed that Queen Obiageli could find a place in her heart to forgive him. King Obeze worried that the confession might worsen her health.

As he made his way to the queen's chambers, he hoped for the best.

CHAPTER TWENTY-THREE

The echoes of the chief priest's voice became music to the ears of King Obeze. Perhaps there was still a chance to redeem himself and to heal his family and the kingdom.

However, the queen's illness remained a mystery, as no herbal potions had been able to relieve her of the ailment, not even the best herbal leaves from Uganka shrine which were known to cure every ailment. Uganka was a land blessed with herbs and medicines. People from different kingdoms travelled far and wide to get a taste of the herbal juice.

The natives of Uganka were also known to be powerful traditional herbalists, passing down skills from one generation to the other.

No one within, around, or outside of the Uganka kingdom had been able to replicate the secret recipe. The herbal juice was discreetly prepared by certified herbalists within the kingdom of Uganka.

Anyone with an ailment that passed through the land of Uganka was healed before the next market day. However, that had not been the case with Queen Obiageli. Some said she was being punished by the gods for falsifying and obscuring the birth of a child.

King Obeze thought about the confession he was about to make to the people. The sound of

Ezemmuo's voice kept resonating in his head. "The gods indeed were awakened the moment King Obeze unknowingly banished his bloodline and his grandchild, the instant he let anger get in the way of his right judgement! Now he must pay the price, for the land needs to be cleansed from all atrocities."

King Obeze imagined the reactions of the people after his confession. He imagined they must have heard about the recent happenings but could only speak in whispers and low tones.

The confession would be the beginning of a new era, or the end of his catastrophic reign.

How could he face the people after his confession? This was a confession he would have loved to say with his wife beside him, but with the queen's failing health, he would have to speak to the people alone.

He was on the verge of losing everything: his wife, his kingdom his son, his grandchild, and maybe the throne.

As the sun rose, the morning breeze blew into the king's sleeping chambers. He awoke with a start, heart pounding.

It was the day of the great confession. He set out for the royal courtyard.

The people were already summoned and assembled there, and amongst them was Ezemmuo and the king's cabinet.

King Obeze arrived, trying to feel and look calm as uncontrollable thoughts and questions, with possibly no definite answers, charged through his mind.

The king made his way to his seat accompanied by two guards, Ebuka and Ikenna, who stood side by side in an erect position. The murmuring crowd became quiet as they waited for the king to speak.

King Obeze cleared his throat, unsure about how to begin. He glanced at Ezemmuo who gestured with a head nod as a signal to start talking.

"My people! The beloved people of our great land, I greet you all," King Obeze spoke in a loud voice.

The people responded with great vocal affirmation.

King Obeze narrated the whole sad history to his people, his voice sometimes faltering, but he spared them no details.

The king further explained to the people how he angered the gods by these lies and deceit and, to make matters worse, by unknowingly banishing his grandchild, whom Sọchima conceived with Erimma.

The people stared in bewilderment; there were loud murmurings amongst the crowd, disappointment darkening their faces.

Realizing they had been living in deceit the whole time, the people's reactions were unprecedented.

As soon as the king was done talking, Ezemmuo walked up to pat him on the shoulder.

The chief priest turned around to address the murmuring crowd. "My people, our king has done the right thing by speaking the truth before you all. In as much as he is the king, he is human too, and he gave in to his weakness and should be forgiven. Remember, he is still our king! We shall all go back to our respective homes! May the gods of our lands keep us all safe!" After Ezemmuo concluded his speech, the people gradually dispersed.

Ezemmuo and the king's cabinet gathered for a quick meeting with King Obeze inside the throne room.

"We shall prepare for the sacrifice to cleanse the land on next eke market day," Ezemmuo spoke as he handed King Obeze a cowry.

"Take it; the cowry is a symbol to show that you have done what is expected of you bravely. Now you should prepare for the rites of cleansing."

 King Obeze accepted the cowry and handed it to Ebuka who placed it carefully in the royal bowl.

While Ezemmuo was getting ready to leave, Udoka, one of the palace guards, the son of Adigwe, ran into the throne room panting like one being chased by a wolf.

Sounding traumatized, he cried, "My king! My king! The queen! Our queen! She has joined her ancestors! She breathes no more!"

The room went dead in silence at the shocking news of the queen's demise.

King Obeze quietly exited the throne room and headed towards the queen's private chambers.

CHAPTER TWENTY-FOUR

The news of the queen's death spread like wildfire with the sound of the ikoro. King Obeze was devastated.

Everyone knew the queen's health was deteriorating, but no one knew that she would join her ancestors on a day such as the day of the great confession.

Allegations bandied around, implying that she had died of heart break, depression from Sọchima's exile, and shame from the great confession.

Ugonna, the queen's royal maiden servant, had found the queen lying helplessly on her wooden bed. When queen Obiageli did not come out for her routine check to tend to her plants, Ugonna knew there was something wrong. No matter how sick Queen Obiageli appeared to be, she never forgot about caring for her plants.

While the scenario surrounding the death of the queen seemed more like a suicidal death, no one dared mentioned the word "suicide," as that was a sacrilegious act in the land of Ogbodo, and anyone caught in that act was thrown into the evil forest with no chance of reincarnation.

If that were the case for Queen Obiageli, even she would be thrown into the evil forest.

The king's cabinet and the king waited patiently for Ezemmuo to commune with the gods.

The people needed to know if the queen died a natural death by giving in to her ailment; or, maybe there was more that the eyes had not seen yet, nor the ears heard. With that in mind, the queen's funeral was put on hold until word came back from Ezemmuo.

If the queen were buried before news came back, and the cause of death was known to be suicide, the queen would have to be dug up and thrown into the evil forest.

No one knew how long it would take for words to come back from the gods. As the people waited patiently, King Obeze grew anxious. He feared for the queen's corpse if the verdict were suicide.

The emptiness and grief that engulfed him caused his body to ache tremendously. I have lost everything, he thought. I have completely failed.

If he had known all would end in this manner, he would not have agreed to the plot in the first place. That may have left him childless with no heir and the loss of the throne, but in exchange he would have had peace and honour.

Now he had lost everything that he tried so hard to protect and acquire.

King Obeze rarely left his chambers. He spent most of the time murmuring words to himself. King Obeze questioned every decision of his life as he paced from one end of the room to another. He was in so much grief and he was afraid to face the people.

He feared confronting his past and living for the future. He had drenched himself in so much alcohol that even a bath would do him no good.

218

Never had he meant nor wished for things to turn out the way they did.

For the first time in his reign, King Obeze Ubaka of Ogbodo felt helpless.

The thought of facing all these consequences alone made him shiver.

It was five market days since the death of Queen Obiageli, yet no word had come from Ezemmuo. Everyone in the kingdom felt nervous and troubled. The tense thoughts and rising uncertainties filled the air. Sooner or later, word would come back from the gods.

As everyone went about their business, the cabinet kinsmen met each day to discuss plans for a possible funeral rite for the queen. If the news came back as a natural cause of death, the queen would have to be buried with funeral rites rushed as quickly as possible.

This would aid to quickly commence the purification and cleansing rites of King Obeze to cleanse and free the land from all the evil intricacies existing within the past years of his kingship.

The purification and cleansing rites were meant to have happened after the king's confession, but with the sudden news of the queen's death, everything was put on hold, especially with the fear of suicide.

The queen's body was being preserved in the sacred shrine of Ogbodo kingdom. No one could see or touch her corpse, not even the king himself. It was believed that anyone who saw a body potentially designated for the evil forest would be inflicted with a curse, since the corpse of a suicidal death was cursed.

Only Ezemmuo could see the queen's body, and only the chief priest could prep the body, at least until the message from the gods proved other than suicide. Two guards were placed at the entrance of the sacred shrine to guard the queen's body.

As the seventh day since the queen's demise approached, Ezemmuo made his presence known with his loud incantations as he headed towards the king's throne room. The king's cabinet and chiefs were already there having a brief meeting.

As Ezemmuo entered, the room suddenly became quiet. The king's cabinet and chiefs all knew that Ezemmuo was back with a message from the gods.

He finished his incantations, opened his purse, and gently placed some cowries on the floor. He stepped over them, and in a loud tone he exclaimed, "Great King of Ogbodo kingdom, your wife, our queen, died of natural causes, but not without a broken heart and a crushed spirit."

The king replied, "Ezemmuo, the great eyes and ears of the gods! As you have spoken, let it be done according to the will of the gods. The queen's body must be prepped and buried, and we shall all continue with the funeral rites."

Word moved quickly like fast tides. The news of Ezemmuo's revelation was spoken all over the lands. The people thanked the gods for averting the consequences that came with a suicidal death.

The trip to the evil forest was something the people dreaded. The last time such trip was made was when Njide the wife of Egboka took her own life because of being barren.

Njide swore that it would be over her dead body to see Egboka marry another wife because of her being childless.

While Egboka thought that Njide was merely ranting like a snake with no poisonous venom, he went ahead and began to prepare to marry a second wife. Egboka did not want to die a childless man or grow old without fathering a child.

However, he did not know of Njide's barrenness until six years into the marriage when Nnejekwu, the midwife from Abaziani, confirmed that she was unable to bear children due to some large perforations around the uterus.

Njide was disappointed at the news, especially since she was a virgin when she married Egboka. That was why she swore it was over her dead body for Egboka to marry a second wife.

The perforations were not a result of an abortion gone wrong, but rather as a result of a surgery procedure gone wrong which she had as a child in order to save her life; Njide did not know the severity of the damage until she married and waited to be pregnant.

Child adoption was not an option, as the child would grow up an outcast and could never own land. Everyone avoided adoption like the plaque. It was said that it was better to die childless than to raise an outcast as your own child.

Egboka loved Njide so much, but he was not prepared to die a childless man. After he married his new bride, Njide ran to the stream of Afocha and drowned herself. While her body was being prepped for the evil forest, Egboka forced his way into the shrine to see Njide's body. After that incident, Egboka suffered mental illness that required psychiatric care.

It was said that the curse was upon him for seeing a body designated for the evil forest.

Egboka's new bride eventually left him, and that was the last time anyone heard of Egboka.

Queen Obiageli was given a very good funeral befitting of a queen. The funeral rites were performed, and she was laid to rest. The event attracted visitors and well-wishers from different communities and kingdoms. It lasted three days, after which the cabinet chiefs and King Obeze quickly put in place preparations for the purification and cleansing rites.

CHAPTER TWENTY-FIVE

The morning of the purification rites approached with a magnificent sunrise of blue and white skies. Birds were chattering, and masquerades were preparing for the big dance, especially the sacred Okpoko masquerade of Ogbodo kingdom.

Ezemmuo and the cabinet chiefs had already assembled in the shrine before the first cock crew. Ibeka, the town crier, had already walked the village square twenty times with the same message of the purification ceremony.

One would think that Ibeka was drunk by the way he would say the same message repeatedly, but it was his job to ensure that the message reached everyone and every household.

The purification rites brought hope to the people of Ogbodo kingdom; they were like an absolution for the people and the lands of Ogbodo to cleanse them from all evil deeds.

Time had quickly sped by—and yet there was no sign of prince Sọchima.

King Obeze feared his son had died alone in the forest of thirst and hunger, a broken leg, an infected wound, or by having been torn to death by wild beasts. The absence of Sọchima meant that there was no heir apparent to the throne, but this was no longer a concern for King Obeze; he simply wanted his son to be safe, to embrace him. Hopelessness consumed the king.

He imagined that, after all these struggles to safeguard the throne so it would remain in the Ubaka lineage, all now was lost.

He had no wife, no child, and no throne.

Life and its existence had lost all appeal for King Obeze.

If only he known things would turn out the way it did, he wouldn't have tried to force the hands of the gods to keep something that was not meant to be kept; that is: the throne of Ogbodo kingdom.

Some nights, King Obeze prayed and wished for death to come, but death would be far from his eyes if the gods did not will it.

However, the purification rites might restore peace to the land and to the people of Ogbodo kingdom.

Kind Obeze had suffered greatly during the past months. He walked the path to the shrine accompanied by Ebuka his personal guard. The people all gathered and waited at the palace courtyard for the return of the king from the purification rites.

As Obeze approached the shrine, Ezemmuo waved the king and his guard to stop. The kinsmen walked the path and escorted Obeze inside the sacred chambers. The sacred Okpoko masquerade was walking through the arena with layers of smoke fuming out of its head. The Okpoko masquerade carried a knife that could slice off three men's heads all at once.

Ezemmuo ended his divine incantations, and the kinsmen along with King Obeze knelt in front of the shrine with their hands on their chests.

Each word from Ezemmuo had the men beating their chests with their right hand molded to a fist.

The king repeated each word Ezemmuo instructed him to. After the chants were over, Ezemmuo poured some freshly perfumed oil on the head of King Obeze.

Ezemmuo damped the oil off with a white cloth and gave it to the king to keep as a sign of the completion of the purification rites and as a seal that the gods have been rightfully appeased.

The ceremony ended with Okpoko masquerade dancing as he moved around the shrine with his knife thrusting downwards to the ground. The people welcomed the king with open arms. They adored his humility and total submission to the will and desires of the gods. The women danced vigorously while the men fought over kegs of palm wine.

The king and his kinsmen made their way back to the village, and the king felt relieved and content. At last, the peace he had always wanted for his people had finally come to pass.

The king felt reborn and new again, his inner peace restored. Now he could focus on working and making things better for his people through practical and transparent governance.

The gods willing, King Obeze believed Sọchima would return home

In as much as the king was happy the kingdom had been restored, he still carried the burden of a troubled and traumatised man within him. Living with the pangs of loneliness and grief was just an additional layer of icing on his cake.

It was indeed a new dawn of a new era for the people of Ogbodo kingdom. Farmlands were beginning to yield crops; trade had been established with other communities including Abaziani. Both communities agreed to live peacefully after the purification rites.

As King Obeze devoured a glass of fresh palm wine, he felt consumed with desire to see his son again and his grandchild, either dead or alive, if only the gods would grant him one last wish.

He thought about his dead wife, Queen Obiageli, and he wished she were there with him. The emptiness he felt was not going away, and he only had a thin thread of hope to hang onto amidst his broken emotions.

King Obeze knew that Prince Sọchima was very upset with him. He had failed Sọchima as a father. A father protects his son regardless; however, Sọchima already knew his father had issues with his first reaction often being anger.

The thought of dying a childless and lonely king was a burden that he wished would disappear. Should the throne be relinquished to another family, he would be remembered as a king who allegedly had an heir but died childless, because no one knew if Sọchima was dead or alive.

King Obeze continued to battle his mental health while fighting his inner demons tirelessly.

It was early in the morning, and a perfect time to walk the path before it became crowded with women and children. The king decided to take a walk through the courtyard to clear his head. He walked over the scattered leaves towards the path leading to the river. This was the path that women and children took for their early morning commute to the river to fetch water.

King Obeze breathed a sigh of relief as the morning wind blew across his face. As the birds chattered above the king's head, his mind returned to the very beginning of his kingship, through to the present day.

He knew it was time! The call was getting stronger and he knew he needed to answer the call.

The voices in his head would not stop talking. They burdened his mind with questions for which he had no answers, the weight of guilt, and fear that he could not overcome. It was difficult to carry this weight alone. As a king, he was expected to be strong and to show no sign of weakness, but that burden was gulping him down like a huge snake.

He felt that no one could understand or take away the weight from him; he had to deal with this alone.

The king knew that living like this was no longer an option for him, for each passing day increased the pain his mind, and he could not make peace with his thoughts.

It was the kind of pain that entitled him to a justifiable death that would free him from the torments of his emotions.

King Obeze carefully drew his sword, which was nicely hidden and properly tucked up inside his flowing garment.

He stared at the sword with fearful eyes. Unseen by anyone, he walked deeper and deeper into the woods close to Amowo stream. Everyone knew the king walked that path when he was in the mood for a walk, so no one followed him. Who would think it was suicide? The king knew he had to make it look like an attack to avoid being thrown into the evil forest.

King Obeze held the sword and slowly struck it right into his chest.

CHAPTER TWENTY-SIX

The hunters and maidens of Abaziani and Ogbodo found King Obeze's unconscious body lying in the bush of Amowo stream. They quickly carried him back to the palace. The king's cabinet chiefs were notified as word spread quickly across the kingdom of the king's sudden condition.

Rumour had it that he was attacked on his morning walk, but who would want to attack him?

Emissaries from Abaziani and other neighbouring kingdoms arrived to pay homage to the king and to wish him well.

Onowu was the leader of the king's cabinet and a second in command, should the king become incapacitated. He ensured that all guests visiting the king were well cared for and attended to. The king was still alive, but in critical condition.

The cabinet chiefs gathered to deliberate on the issues at hand and on what should be done going forward, should events take a worse turn.

The people of Ogbodo kingdom were beginning to gather in the courtyard with inquiries as to the condition of the king.

Ezemmuo returned to the palace to administer herbs to King Obeze, and he was accompanied by a dashing young man with the charisma of a hunter and warrior. The young man looked dazed as he stared across the room. The cabinet chiefs stared back at him as though seeing a ghost.

No one said a word, as they thought it may be the ghost of Sọchima coming to take his father's spirit to the ancestral land; no one knew if Sọchima was dead or alive. They all knew the dashing young man resembled the prince. Ezemmuo guided the young man inside king Obeze's inner chambers accompanied by the cabinet chiefs.

The young man knelt over King Obeze's bed as Ezemmuo touched the king's toes, saying, "My king, behold your son! The prince of Ogbodo kingdom: Prince Sọchima Ubaka."

King Obeze was still unconscious. Prince Sọchima put his hands across his father's head and cried, "I am here, Father, please wake up!"

Ezemmuo narrated to the cabinet chiefs how Sọchima came to him at the shrine as he was preparing herbs for the king. Prince Sọchima heard about the tragedy that befell the king, his father.

Ezemmuo narrated how Sọchima survived the forests until he made his way back to Abaziani where he found Erimma who had now born him a son, and how both lived in Abaziani. They both feared to return home in case the child may be hurt and, since Erimma was still banished, they all decided to stay away.

"Erimma's banishment was lifted the moment the purification rites were completed," Ezemmuo told the prince.

"Where is the child and woman now?" Elder Ibeka asked.

"They are in the courtyard amongst the crowd," Prince Sọchima replied in a tear-filled voice.

Ezemmuo left the king's inner chambers accompanied by Prince Sọchima and the cabinet chiefs. As soon as Ezemmuo made a commanding entrance into the courtyard, the people feared he may be coming with bad news about King Obeze's condition.

Ezemmuo said, "Great people of Ogbodo kingdom! Indeed, the gods act in mysterious ways, for beside me here is our Prince Sọchima, a true son of this great kingdom! He is accompanied by his son and Erimma."

Ezemmuo nodded at Prince Sọchima to get his child and Erimma. He walked into the crowd and came out with Erimma and a boy child.

The people were excited but kept their voices quiet as they did not yet know the outcome of the king's health.

"The little boy, your son! What name have you given to him?" Ezemmuo asked Prince Sọchima.

"Udogazie Ubaka," Sọchima replied with a smile.

In a loud voice, Ezemmuo yelled out, "People of Ogbodo kingdom, welcome the king's grandson, Udogazie Ubaka."

The people screamed louder; now the noise from the courtyard was sufficient to raise the dead.

"Udogazie, my son, it's time for you to meet your grandfather! Come, my son!"

Ezemmuo carried the boy child as he returned to the king's inner chambers with Prince Sọchima and Erimma.

"My son, I was never in support of your father sending Erimma away, especially since you owned up to the pregnancy. Your courage was great, my son; our ways are not the ways of the gods."

Ezemmuo handed the child over to Erimma.

"You are welcome back, my daughter."

Erimma nodded calmly and smiled.

Prince Sọchima took his father's hands and placed them on Udogazie's hands.

"Father, here is your grandson, Udogazie! Erimma is here too! We are sorry for staying away for too long. I forgive you, Father! We can all be a family again with a fresh start. I still love Erimma, and she is now the mother of my child; I know you can hear me. With your blessing, I will make her my wife."

Sọchima was breathing hard with tension.

King Obeze's body lay alive but motionless. As Ezemmuo administered the herbs, the king weakly held Sọchima, Erimma and Udogazie's hands together and gave a weak squeeze.

King Obeze the Great of Ogbodo kingdom breathed his last and died.

Ezemmuo knew the king was gone. He bent over to Sọchima who was already wailing hard as he buried his head on the king's lifeless body.

"My son, your father heard you! He knows you are here now, and he is happy his family is reunited," Ezemmuo said persuasively, patting Sọchima's back.

Ezemmuo notified the king's cabinet chiefs of the demise of the king as they were all waiting in the throne room for news of the king's health.

They all removed their red caps as a sign of respect and walked in a single file to the king's chambers to pay their last respects.

Ezemmuo strolled down to the courtyard to inform the people of the king's death.

He concluded, "As the gods have willed, King Obeze died a happy man. Do not spend so much time in grief and in pain, as we all have a funeral, marriage, and a coronation to plan."

As soon as Ezemmuo finished speaking, the sound of the ikoro filled the air.